A Snap of Magic

A Snap of Secrets

A Snap of Fate

DANIELLE KEIL

Also By Danielle Keil

A Snap of Magic

CHAPTER 1

"Wow, don't go overboard or anything. I almost didn't recognize you. You really went all out this year, huh?" Ezra said as he joined me, sounding a little out of breath. The crisp October air blew leaves over the sidewalk, crunching under our shoes as we made our way to school.

The two of us should have walked together from the start, yet Ezra found it impossible to leave his house on time. Despite only living two homes away, he still had to catch up with me a block or so later.

I raised my coffee cup as a greeting, ignoring his snarky comments. They were the same ones he made every year.

"I like to call it being consistent, thank you very much." I pulled the black cape around my torso tighter so it didn't accidentally get wrapped around Ezra. The silky cape cascaded to my knees, but the smallest gust of wind blew it around like a plastic bag floating in the air.

"I call it lack of creativity, but that's fine."

I raised an eyebrow and shot him a look, though I knew he was joking. "Oh? And what are you supposed to be, a bully? You're doing a fine job at that. Did you really even need a costume?"

That got Ez to snort out a laugh. He pushed his dark-rimmed glasses further up his nose and grinned. "Actually, I am a bully. I'm Sid from Toy Story." He gestured down at his black T-shirt with a skull on it, over a long white sleeved shirt. "Fisher is going as Andy and decided I needed to dress up accordingly, even before trick-or-treating."

The desperate need to give Ezra's seven-year-old little brother a high five right now was overwhelming. The little guy and I got along amazingly well, but this? Top tier level. Ezra hadn't dressed up for Halloween in almost five years, since before high school. Actually getting him in a costume, no matter how close to normal clothes it was, required a large amount of skill.

And probably a massive bribe. I wondered if it was Fisher or Ezra's mom that currently dangled some sort of forbidden fruit over Ezra's head at the moment.

"Well, I might be in the same hat and costume, but at least I changed the outfit underneath." I went with a fall slash Halloween theme for my outfit this year, a rusty orange loose crop top over a black and white striped long-sleeved shirt I had tucked into my bra so it didn't hang under the crop top.

"You wore those jeans yesterday," Ezra pointed out, gesturing to my ripped up baggy jeans. I had to fold the bottom hems a few times, as I was a bit too short for them to go full length, even though I had on my favorite purple Doc Martens for an extra few inches.

I took one last swig of my coffee, draining the cup as we turned onto the path to head into school.

"That's not the—hey!" A huge blast of wind swooped down over us, taking my witch's hat with it. "Come back!" It flew behind me, tumbling down the sidewalk we just passed over. A few seconds later, it fell still, flopping over to the side.

I shoved my mug into Ezra's hands and ran after it, picking it up by the tip and dusting it off before shoving it back onto my head.

With a huff, my jaw set, and now not in a great mood, I marched back to my best friend and took my cup. "Honestly, why is it always me?"

Ezra laughed and patted my shoulder. "It's the law of commonalities."

My nose scrunched. "That's not a thing."

"Okay, it might not be the name for it, but it's when people group things together, especially negative things. You think things like your hat," he reached up and tapped the top, "is something that is bad and always happens to you. Because your brain usually only remembers the negative things like that."

"Yeah, but even you have to realize things like that *do* always happen to me. My hat. Spilling orange juice all over my jeans last week so it looked like I peed myself. Anything that happens in Chem lab. The time the seagull pooped on my head at the zoo."

Ezra held open the large, heavy front doors and ushered me inside with a shrug. "True, but those things were all spread out. I bet you could poll anyone and they could come up with a small list of random things that also happen to them over a long period of time."

I rolled my eyes. "Why don't you ever let me just wallow in my own pity?"

"Because the sun shines another day, rockstar." Ezra grinned, his cheeks pushing up his glasses slightly. His ridiculously messy hair flopped over his forehead, making him look younger than he was. We both turned eighteen two weeks ago, on the same day, yet he looked like he wasn't even old enough to drive sometimes.

Then there was me. With my long, rusty reddish-brown hair and bright green eyes, people have always been telling me I looked older than I was. Now that I was eighteen, I could officially say, "I'm an adult," without sounding snobby. Even if I was still in high school.

"Another day I wished I had a magic wand and could make all the back luck disappear," I whispered as we reached my locker. "One flick of the wrist, and hat would stay on head, OJ would stay in the bottle, and poop would stay in the seagull."

Ezra tilted his head, then lifted the back of his hand to my forehead. He didn't have to lift far, as he was already six feet tall and I was a good seven inches shorter. "You okay? It's not like you to be so down, especially on your favorite holiday."

I sighed, dropping my backpack at my feet and leaning back against the cool metal. "Yeah, I'm good. Bummed about the carnival and getting the lame booth, though. And that you're missing it."

My best friend gave me a tight-lipped smile. "Sorry. Fisher wants to get a head start on trick-or-treating tonight. But I'll be there for movie—whoops! Gotta go!" The bell rang mid-sentence, and he was off like a light.

Rolling my eyes again, I turned to my locker and got what I needed to start the day. Ezra was right; it was Halloween, my favorite holiday.

Forget the hat. Forget the booth. I was determined to have fun today, as always.

Chapter 2

"Don't forget, the *entire* packet is due tomorrow!" Mrs. Grey shouted over the sound of the bell, two dozen students packing up their things, chairs scraping on the floor, and an overall scuffle to get out of the classroom.

In unison, everyone groaned, myself included.

"Mrs. Grey, it's *Halloween*. The carnival is tonight. Can't we push it off by one day?" Jack asked, holding his hands clasped together under his chin and batting his eyelashes at our teacher. It didn't quite work the way he planned, though, mostly because he was dressed like the Kool-Aid man, giant red pitcher and all. It was hard to take him seriously.

But Mrs. Grey didn't budge. "Assigning you all this for tonight will ensure that no one has time to go out and get into trouble. Halloween is notorious for teenagers getting themselves into trouble, and I will not stand for it." Her demeanor went well with what some would have considered a costume, if they had not known she wore almost the same thing every day. With her long, gray hair wrapped up in a severely tight bun at the nape of her neck, glasses perched on the end of her nose held in place with a long chain, and a flowered dress, she looked like she was dressed the part of 'stereotypical grandmother.'

Except it was her every day look and she wasn't the warm and sweet grandmother who slipped you ten dollars and candy when your parents weren't looking.

"I actually have to take my little sister trick-or-treating after the carnival," Jack said, his hands now at his side, a frown on his face.

That was true. Jack and his sister came to my house every year. They were one of only about five people that did, and it was probably because their dad was friendly with Gramps. Friend*ly*, not friends. No one was really friends with Gramps. He was a grumpy old man, just shy of telling people to get off his lawn. Sometimes I even called him Grumps instead of Gramps.

He didn't find it as funny as I did.

My hat caught on the doorway as I left the room, knocking it askew. I reached up to adjust it as I sidestepped past a zombie cheerleader making out with a werewolf with hairy paws. I wondered if he kept those on while taking notes in class, and how he would eat lunch without getting fur in his mouth.

I shook my head, laughing to myself. Halloween was chaos at DeBruin High.

The whole town of DeBruin took Halloween seriously. Sometimes a little *too* seriously. We went all out for this specific holiday. While some towns made magical, wonderful Christmas displays, or put their budget into Fourth of July firework shows, we spent ours on Halloween.

The DeBruin High School carnival was the kickoff. It started right after school and lasted well into the night for older kids and adults. Once the booths shut down, the younger kids headed home for trick-or-treating. But the adults could stay for the haunted house, the rides, and more.

The high schoolers also got credit for working the carnival, which was the reason most of us did it. No job was too big or too small, said the teachers. Unless you were crowned King or Queen, because yes, we also had that.

The titles always went to seniors, which meant this year I was eligible. Not that I expected it by a long shot or even wanted it, but it had to be better than running the 'Take your chance at a Halloween duck' booth.

Spending hours painting yellow duckies into terrifying creatures wasn't all that bad, though. I made a handful into zombies, coloring them green and making it look like their faces were falling off. Some I turned into gargoyles, making them all gray and stone like. A handful became vampires, with pointy teeth and red eyes. Then there were the less terrifying ones, like princesses, witches, cats, and my personal favorite, the yellow duck.

I left one duck as is. Like the guy who comes to school on Halloween with a t-shirt that reads 'this is my costume.' There's always one person who refuses to dress up, or does the bare minimum. So for this carnival, yellow duck came to work as a yellow duck. When among an entire pond full of masked ducks, he didn't even stand out. It was genius. To me, at least.

If I was going to have the lamest booth, the least I could do was entertain myself. Because it was so lame, it was a one person booth, which meant I didn't even get to hang out with anyone during the carnival. *And*, since Gramps refused to answer the door, I also didn't get to stay for the after hours fun.

At least I had the movie marathon to look forward to.

"What's on the list for tonight?" Ezra magically appeared at my side, even though I had been expecting him. We always intersected between hallways C and F at this time of day, traveled down C Hall, where we would part at the next intersection, only to come back together at lunch.

"I was thinking a romance, actually." I grinned, trying to make my face seem less suspicious. The two of us had been having a scary movie marathon on Halloween for a few years now, and it was my turn to choose the movies. I picked the perfect one, without too many jump scares for Ezra.

We didn't need a repeat of two years ago, when we went through five bags of popcorn because he kept jerking the bowl every jump scare and spilling popcorn all over the floor.

Ezra adjusted his glasses and blinked a few times. "Cecilia, it's Halloween, remember? Doesn't that mean—actually, you know what, no. It's fine. A romance it is. Great choice. Which one were you thinking? When Harry Met Sally? Sleepless in Seattle? Never Been Kissed?"

"First off, why are all your suggestions absolutely ancient? But no." I tapped a chipped nail polish topped index finger to my chapped lips, pretending to think. "I was thinking more of a romance... with chainsaws."

Ezra groaned and hung his head. "I knew it was too good to be true," he whispered under his breath. "Texas Chainsaw Massacre?"

I nodded enthusiastically, my hair bobbing in a braid down my back. "Yup. Every single one of them. At least, as many as we can make it through."

"We do have school tomorrow," he reminded me. That meant his curfew was eleven and not midnight, even though it was a holiday. The good thing was that he lived so close that he could leave at eleven and still make it home at eleven.

"I solemnly swear I'll have all my homework done before you come over," I answered, crossing my fingers behind my back while using my other hand to mark an X on my chest.

He knew it was a total and complete lie and I would probably spend more time after he left doing homework than before, but it didn't matter. Either way, the work got done.

"See you later," he called as he turned left and I went right.

I dodged a guy dressed as a bloody butcher with a fake knife in his skull and some sort of Star Trek character as I made my way to Chemistry, my least favorite class. All the memorizing of letters and numbers as well as having to do math? At least one time, our teacher let us make candy while learning. That had been a good day.

Today seemed like it could be on par with that. As I pushed through the door, I immediately noticed a small smoking cauldron sitting on each lab table.

"Greetings, witches and wizards," a voice came floating behind a larger cauldron in the back of the room.

We all eagerly took our seats, awaiting what was next. I had never been excited about Chemistry before, but today looked like fun.

"Can we eat this?" someone called out. I couldn't see what he was holding up, but considering 'Do not eat' was on the list of commandments in the front of the room, I was pretty sure the answer was going to be no.

"Yes!" my teacher called. Also dressed as a witch, she put my costume to shame. Mrs. Chung had on the full shebang—green and purple striped tights, pointy boots, a black dress with spiderweb details, cape, hat, and even a wart on her nose, which was painted green, as was the rest of her face. She held a broom in one hand, her safety goggles in the other.

"Just not yet," she continued as she walked between the lab tables. "You need to brew it first."

I stared at the smoking cauldron in front of me. So far, most of the experiments I did tended to... not work. Chemistry didn't seem to be my strong suit, so I didn't expect 'brewing potions' would be any easier.

Mrs. Chung put the directions on each table and set us to work. She had already concocted half of the potion; it was up to us to finish it. She said we could drink it once she inspected it. "And not a moment before," she warned, giving us a stare down.

I looked across the lab table at my partner, my friend, Matt. Together, we made a horrible team, because neither of us was well skilled in this particular subject. Throw me in art, I'd do fine. P.E? Sure. Heck, I'd even excel in World History better than Chemistry. Same with Matt.

He gave me a weary smile, his braces gleaming in the fluorescent lighting. He had to pull his hair back in a shower cap since it fell past his chin, but wasn't long enough to pull back like mine. Another lab rule.

"Should we put our safety goggles on?" I asked, pushing his pair across the table.

"Yes, we should always be prepared—"

"For something to go wrong," I finished for him. It was the same thing we said at the start of every lab period, because inevitably something *did* go wrong. Which made me even more nervous about today.

CHAPTER 3

"Ewwww," I groaned, lifting my hand away from my shirt, a long, sticky, slimy green glob stretching between my right palm and my left arm. "It's like a troll sneezed all over me."

Mrs. Chung tsked in our direction. "Not exactly how that potion was supposed to brew, CC."

I gave her a pained smile. "I figured. It doesn't look like I could even drink this if I tried. Maybe if you have a knife and fork?" The goop wasn't really thick enough to cut, but it made her smile. It looked more like those giant tubs of slime that came with all the mix-ins and scents. Ezra's little brother had about a dozen of them.

Matt had somehow managed to jump out of the way before he got slimed, so it was just me who had to deal with the green goop all over my shirt and partially on my face.

"Go get yourself cleaned up. I'll see you tomorrow," Mrs. Chung said with a sympathetic look. It wasn't the first time I had been excused from her class to fix something I messed up. But honestly, how was I supposed to know that adding the ingredients in the wrong order would make it explode and not sizzle? They were listed right next to each other; I just put one in before the other. The wrong way, apparently.

Matt said his goodbyes and promised to visit me at the carnival. I was going to hold him to that, since I assumed my booth would be the quietest and I would be bored out of my mind.

I went to change out of my long sleeve shirt and crop top and into a plain black T-shirt I randomly had in my locker. After giving it a quick sniff test, I deemed it worthy enough to wear, even if I would be slightly chilly at the carnival later. At least I could wrap my cape around me if I needed.

The rest of the day went ridiculously normal. Almost *too* normal, especially for it being Halloween. Sure, people were dressed up, and a few tried pulling some harmless pranks, but other than that, nothing happened.

Except the candy. My bag was full of candy from teachers and random students throwing it around in the halls. That was the best part of Halloween, hands down. Now I would have something to munch on while sitting all alone at my booth.

Ezra met up with me at my locker at the end of the day, attempting to see if I had changed my mind on my choice of movie.

"Can I suggest a less scary one? Maybe Hocus Pocus or Nightmare Before Christmas?" he asked, batting his eyelashes behind his oversized glasses.

"Nope, sorry. I get to choose this year, and the list is set. Be at my house by seven and don't—"

"Ring the bell, I know."

Gramps hated the doorbell, yet he would never let me take it down. He refused to dismantle it under the assumption that Mom would come back one day. His worst fear was that she would show up and he wouldn't hear someone knocking on the door, and she would leave. No matter how many times I tried to convince him that was the furthest thing from reality, he stuck to it.

I, however, had accepted reality long ago. Mom left when I was born and she wasn't coming back. She had eighteen years to reappear, and so far, it hadn't happened. Over time, Gramps made up excuses about why Mom left that varied every time he spoke about it.

According to him, Mom had found a new guy and jumped on the back of his motorcycle and took off one day. Then, it was the mafia, and she was in witness protection. Another time, she bought a one-way plane ticket to Europe and never looked back. Once, he said she was kidnapped by witches and taken hostage somewhere in Rhode Island.

Each time, he came up with something more and more outlandish. I wasn't sure if it was his memory leaving him or if he did it so I wouldn't ever know the truth. There was the other option where *he* didn't know the truth either.

I pushed through the back doors of school and out toward the practice football field and parking lot, where the Halloween carnival took place.

The air buzzed with excitement, a flurry of chatter and the screams of delights of the early attendees hanging over my head.

The booths and rides had been set up over the last few days, but now that it was go time, the place exploded in a myriad of anarchy.

People in costumes ducked and dodged everywhere, trying to avoid running into each other as everyone carried boxes with last-minute items, prizes, candy, or décor.

Food vendors fired up their trucks and booths, the delicious smells traveling across the way, hitting my nose at just the right time for me to take a deep breath and let out a sigh of satisfaction. The fragrant smell of deep-fried corn dogs, elephant ears, greasy pizza slices and gooey caramel apples made my mouth water.

Large poles held up twinkle lights and strings of small globe lights crisscrossing overhead. After dark, it would look like the night sky had been lowered down to us. Spiderwebs draped over everything, all sizes of spiders hanging down from their threads.

My booth was on the far side, away from most of the craziness, but close to a popcorn stand. The buttery aroma of the fresh popped popcorn mixed with the crisp, cool air of the afternoon.

There was nothing remarkable about my booth, though—it was a wooden stand with 'Ducks' painted on the top. Every year, it got disassembled and put into storage for next year. This time, I had the distinct pleasure of repainting the entire booth and the sign. I recruited my friend Miranda, who didn't have a booth to paint and had better artistic skills, to help though.

When I got there, thankful it had been put together by someone other than me, because that would have been a disaster waiting to happen, I rounded around the back and dropped my stuff off to the side. Then I headed to inspect the game, making sure the pool had been filled and all my ducks were in a row. Literally.

The pool was a little kiddie pool, sitting onto a folding table right at the edge of the booth. Participants would hand me their ticket, then lean over and grab one of my immaculately painted Halloween ducks, flipping it over to see the colored dot on the bottom. The dot corresponded to a certain level of prizes, which currently hung on both side walls. The prizes ranged from small fidgets, bags of candy, and noise makers all the way to a giant stuffed ghost.

"CC!" someone squealed from my right.

I whirled around, my cape getting caught on the corner of the folding table as I did. I yanked on it to get it free, but it wouldn't budge. I took a step forward to try to unhook it from whatever it was snagged on, but it was *stuck* stuck.

"Cecilia, are you—"

One more yank and I was finally free. With a two-inch gash in my cape.

And the entire pool of ducks sliding toward me.

"No, no, no!" I shrieked, holding my cape over my face like that was going to protect me. The last yank somehow sent the pool over the edge of the table, sending a wave of water and ducks at my feet.

I dropped the cape and reached for the pool, trying to pull it up to salvage enough water that people could still play. But in doing so, I over compensated, and more water came sloshing off as it careened over the other side, once again soaking my jeans, socks, and shoes.

Somehow, I had managed to ruin almost every part of my outfit except my hat today.

"CC!" Miranda finally appeared at my side, her hands over her mouth, covering her shock. "What happened?"

In true Miranda fashion, she painted her nails perfectly to match her booth. She was in charge of the 'pop the balloon on the ghost' one and had all ten nails as little ghosts.

"Umm..." I stared at the now empty pool hanging half of the table like a limp noodle, all the ducks I painted over the last three weeks scattered around on the soggy grass. "I'm not even sure. But my legs are very wet."

She looked down, seeing my jeans sopping wet from the knee down, my Docs basically small ponds of water. The laugh that escaped wasn't unexpected.

"I'm so sorry. It's not funny. It's really not. Your booth is... Well, I think you might be out of a job." She couldn't hide the smile on her face, and neither could I.

"I'm not sure if that's a good thing or a bad thing. But I really could use a change of clothes. For the second time today."

"Matt told me about Chemistry..."

I shrugged. Once again, nothing new for me. Trouble seemed to find me no matter where I went. At least, it was usually trouble for me and not for others.

The DJ started playing music then, which was the cue that the carnival would start in just a few minutes. Everyone gasped, looking up and holding their breath for a moment, realizing the time. Then, in an instant, everyone scrambled about, shouting last-minute instructions, draping cloths over their tables, and finalizing all their work.

The carousel whirred to life, the familiar melody echoing through the air. The carnival was a cherished tradition in this town, a nostalgic celebration for everyone.

More sounds of Halloween rushed forward, from the creepy background music to the chimes of winning games, as I panicked over what to do. I couldn't leave everything like this, not if I wanted to get the credit for working. Besides, an empty booth was a bad look, and I wasn't going to be the one who deserted it.

"Quick, help me put the ducks back," I said hurriedly. They wouldn't be floating in the pool, but I could still at least have people pick them up for a prize.

Miranda and I made fast work of getting them into the pool, sitting correctly on the table, before she sprinted back to her booth three rows over and out of sight.

The chair provided for me was wet. The grass under me was wet. Not wanting to stand in soggy socks any longer, I took them and my shoes off, squishing my toes on the damp ground. Then, I went around the side and stood in front of the booth, wanting some dry ground to stand on for a bit. If someone came, I would hurry back.

Since my booth was one of the furthest from the entrance to the carnival, I knew it would be a while before someone came, *if* anyone came at all. There was nothing all that exciting about picking up a rubber duck and seeing if it had a certain color circle on the bottom of it. The prizes weren't all that great either, except for the stuffed ghost. The special duck had a purple dot under her and was the one I made into a witch with the wart on her nose.

At least the music was decent this year. It was a new DJ, as last years had been fired for playing the same six songs over and over again.

This guy kept up the beat, hyping up the crowd, and setting the vibe. He played more fun, upbeat music, danceable music. I tapped my shoeless feet on the ground, willing myself not to break out my dance moves in front of everyone. But I couldn't stop myself from drumming my hands on my thighs and snapping along in some parts. The songs were really that catchy.

He even had some I hadn't heard in *years*, bringing a smile to my face at the memory of me and Gramps walking around the carnival as a little girl. Memories filled my mind, from the sticky cotton candy all over my face, to winning prize after prize, even if Gramps had to cheat a little. My favorite booth had been the water gun vampire race, where Gramps and I shot the water pistols into the small hole, which raised the cartoon looking vampire picture up to his coffin.

The one booth I had never visited was the duck booth. Figured.

But right now, I saw someone headed my way. Butterflies hit my stomach, my nerves waking up, a shiver spreading through my body. I turned around to make sure everything was set and I was ready to go. There was no doubt that I would get multiple comments about the pool not being filled, but—

But...

But...

I stood in shock, my jaw dropped, my breath caught in my throat.

The pool was filled. Like it had been a few minutes ago, before disaster struck. All the little duckies were floating, swimming in circles, and crashing into their friends. A gargoyle about kissed a zombie, and my one normal yellow duck was surrounded by witches.

I looked up, glancing around to see if someone had come by with a giant bucket of water when I hadn't been looking. Surely I would have heard it, right? How could someone have filled up an entire inflatable pool without my knowledge? It wasn't big by any means, more so one that would have held some drinks or something, but it still took more than a cup of water to fill it.

There was no one there, though. Maybe I had been so engrossed with the music that I didn't hear the water being poured. Someone must have seen what happened and ran to get more before the carnival started.

Probably Janet. She was in charge of the entire thing and had an eye on everything all the time. Nothing happened at the Halloween carnival without Janet's approval or knowledge.

That had to be it.

Janet saved the day.

Too bad she couldn't dry my pants, though.

CHAPTER 4

Since today was a gorgeous day in DeBruin, the late October air brisk, but not too cold, I decided not to be lazy and walk home after the carnival ended. Normally, Miranda would give me a ride, but she wanted to stick around for the after hours fun, while I had to go answer the door for trick-or-treaters.

I even took the scenic route for my walk, spending the extra few minutes outside. Given that it was Halloween, I figured going past the cemetery would be a fun added bonus to the holiday.

A bunch of little kids sprinted by me, their plastic pumpkins swinging besides them as their shrieks filled the air. I grinned as I slipped my oversized headphones on and pressed play on my phone. I waved to them on beat, bopping my head and doing a small dance.

The temperature dropped as soon as I got to the gates of the cemetery. I shivered as a chilly gust of wind passed over me.

"Very funny, Mother Nature," I whispered to myself while pulling my cape around me tightly. "Showing off a little as soon as I reached the graveyard? Are you celebrating Halloween too?"

Thankfully, no one was around to witness me talking to an imaginary person.

The song switched and a new feeling took over me. My feet shuffled as I tapped my hands on my thighs, my lips pursing to whistle to the tune.

Another blast of air blew right past me, headed toward the cemetery this time. At the same time, my hands started tingling. I cursed the darn green goop for ruining my shirt earlier, forcing me to stay in a T-shirt for the rest of the day. If I had my long sleeves on, I would be warmer and not starting to freeze.

I rubbed my hands together while tucking my cape into my elbows in an attempt to keep my arms warm. But then, the song hit the chorus, and I had to go all out, twirling in circles, lifting my hands in the air, and clapping along. When it died down, I rolled my wrists, snapping to the beat. My shoes let out a gross *squish* with every step and stomp, but it wasn't enough to stop me from dancing.

Snap, twirl, stomp.

Snap, snap, twirl, boogie.

Snap, twirl, stomp.

Snap, snap, twirl, boog—

Just then, the front gates to the cemetery flung open, slamming against the fence, then crashing back together in the middle.

I jumped a foot in the air, startled by the loud noises and the sudden movement. My heart leapt into my throat; I could feel the pounding all the way in my ears.

Ezra was the one who got spooked easily, not me. But something like this? Everyone experienced jump scares in their life, but I was smart enough to know there had to be a source behind it.

Did someone forget to lock up tonight? They never kept the cemetery open on Halloween. For a town that was so pro-Halloween, they knew enough to block off access to places that might get harmed during the holiday.

I tiptoed closer to the gates, my hand outstretched just in case they flung open again. It must have been another breeze that made them fly. That, and the—

Huh. That was weird. The closer I got to the gates, now closed, the more I noticed the lock. A giant padlock connected the chain slung around both sides of the fence.

There was no way it could have opened and closed back together like this.

Except... hadn't it? I about jumped out of my skin when the massive metal gates smashed into the fence posts before slamming shut again. They definitely had opened. Maybe when they crashed back together, the chain whipped around, but the padlock? Being closed? That made no sense.

The craziness of Halloween must have gotten to me. I shook my head, trying to pretend none of this happened. Between the ridiculousness of Chemistry and the carnival, today was way too weird.

Turning back to the street, I restarted my music and continued on my way. I was only a block from home now. I had no idea what was going on, but I also didn't want to stick around to find out.

I wasn't one to shy away from the Halloween spookiness. It was one of my favorite holidays of the year. But that... that I couldn't explain.

Once I made it inside, I sighed, leaning my back against the door. My fingers tingled again, finally getting warm after being in the cold air.

I shook them out, clenching and unclenching my fists to get the blood flow going.

"Cecilia? Is that you?" Gramps called from the living room. Like it would be anyone else.

I rolled my eyes. "No, Gramps, it's a serial killer come to rob your house and leave your mutilated, dismembered body in a trail leading to the basement where I plan to wait for Cecilia to come home and catch her in my trap."

Gramps snorted, but not in a way where he found my comment funny. More in a 'you're bothering me' sort of way. He loved me, but we were such complete opposites, it was hard to believe we were family sometimes.

I always wondered if I had gotten Mom's sense of humor, or if she was the same kind of stuffy as Gramps. I would never know, though, because Mom was an off-limits topic for him, unless he brought her up first, which was rare.

"You're on candy duty tonight," he called, ignoring my comments completely.

"I'm always on candy duty," I shot back. I made my way to the kitchen to grab a snack, but turned around a second later, remembering something. "Oh, hey, some lady from the carnival wanted me to tell you hi. What was her name..." I looked up at the ceiling, snapping my fingers until I remembered. "Right, it was—"

Before I could say it, the front door flew open, slamming into the wall behind it, a burst of wind taking out the mail Gramps had dropped onto the front table earlier today.

I shrieked, Gramps gasped, and we both turned toward the door.

"How many times have I told you to make sure that door is closed, child? It's an old house. The frames have settled and now the jambs are all out of sorts. You need to double check," Gramps said grumpily as he pushed to his feet and shuffled over to the door, closing it, jiggling the handle, then locking it for extra safety.

Except I *had* closed it. I had pushed my entire body against it only a minute ago.

I stared down at my hands in wonder. That was twice now that a door or gate flew open. I thought back to the cemetery—what had I been doing right before the gate went crazy? If it even had...

Music. I had been snapping, stomping, twirling, and dancing. But the only thing I had been doing right now was snapping my fingers.

Lifting my right hand, I rolled my wrist and snapped once.

Nothing happened.

I glanced around the room to make sure I didn't miss a cabinet open or something, but nothing budged.

I tried again, snapping once more, with my left hand this time, even though my snaps were weaker on that side.

"What are you doing, child?" Gramps asked, suddenly appearing next to me and grabbing my hand, pushing it down.

"I... I... I was just... and the door... I thought..."

"Well don't," he cracked sharply. But when I looked at him, I found his face pale, a frown settled on his lips. He combed his thin hair to one side, and all of his wrinkles seemed deeper than before. At the same time, his bright blue eyes caught mine, him staring intently at me like he wanted to scold me. Immediately I was brought back to my childhood, when he would reprimand me for a trivial issue, then give me a small smile to reassure me that he wasn't *too* mad.

This time, though, the smile didn't come. How could he be so upset over something I didn't even do? Surely the way he just said the door frame was old and off center meant it wasn't my fault.

"That was weird, though, right? I mean, I did close the door, and..." I tried to vocalize my thoughts, but the second the words left my lips, the more absurd they sounded.

What, did I think I was some sort of witch who could open doors with a snap of my fingers? What was next, taking the trash out with a stomp of my foot? Making my bed with a fart?

It was ridiculous. I was being silly. I was letting Halloween get to me, that was all. It was a windy night outside. All the little witches tonight would have a hard time keeping their pointy hats on, that was for sure.

Which reminded me—it was time to change into my full costume. Which, conveniently, was still a witch, just without the normal teenager clothes on under the cape.

"Nevermind. I'll go change and man the door." Gramps dropped my hand and grunted, shuffling his way to the kitchen no doubt for an old fashioned to drink while he settled in front of the TV in the den.

I jogged upstairs and found the parts of my costume on my bed where I left them this morning. I wasn't a dress up for school kind of Halloween person, but I liked to do it for the kids who came to the door.

When we were younger, Ezra and I would go out searching for candy ourselves. But once we became teens, we found it to be too juvenile and switched to scary movie marathons instead. At least, I did. Sometimes Ezra didn't join because he got sucked into taking his little brother trick-or-treating around the wealthy neighborhood a few minutes away, then claimed exhaustion after.

I slipped my purple striped shirt on, then fitted the plum corset over it. After that, I shimmied my way into matching shorts, striped thigh-high socks, and the cutest brown boots that came up to my calf. I actually wore these a lot throughout the fall, but they were a perfect addition to the costume.

The rip on my cape would have to wait to be mended until later. I managed to undo my braid and fluff my dark auburn hair over my shoulders right as the bell rang for the first time. I rushed down, needing to get there before they rang again, as Gramps *hated* that dang doorbell. Since I hadn't been home long, I hadn't put the 'please knock' sign up yet, like I did every Halloween.

Three hours, a record number of seven trick-or-treaters, and one homework packet later, I was done for the night.

So was Ezra, apparently.

Ezra: Sorryyyyyyy. Had to take Fisher out this year. I also think I messed up my ankle crossing the street, so I'm going to stay home.

Me: Coward.

Ezra: No, I'm fine thanks. I don't think it's broken or sprained. Just twisted.

Me: Wuss.

Ezra: Just some rest will work, but I appreciate your concern. Honestly, your empathy is admirable.

Me: I'll see you tomorrow. Gotta tell you about some weird things that happened tonight.

Ezra: It's Halloween. Everything is weird today.

Me: This was *extra* weird. Not Halloween related.

If anyone would be able to figure out what was going on with me, it would be Ezra. He always had the logical answers to things I went off the rails in delusional land about.

I took my hat off, laying it gently on my desk, and flopped onto the bed. While staring at the ceiling, I tried to summon the witchy powers of Halloween once more with a snap, wondering if maybe my bedroom door would fly open or something.

Nothing. I sighed, out of ideas.

Maybe it really was the wind.

Chapter 5

"Then, when I passed by the gates, they flew open so hard, they bounced off the fence behind it," I said to Ezra as we walked into school the next morning. My arms flung to the side, almost taking him out as they smacked into his chest.

The costumes had died down among the students, everyone back in their normal clothes, although one freshman still looked a little green. I wasn't sure if it was from some bad costume makeup or too much candy the night before.

"So you're saying... What *are* you saying?" Ezra asked as he pushed his glasses up further on his nose. A gaggle of girls rushed by, going around and through the two of us. Ezra narrowly escaped, bumping into me and dropping all the books and papers in his hands.

"I'm *saying*," I lowered my voice so no one could overhear as I knelt down to help him gather his things, "that I think I caused it. It happened again when I got home, with the front door."

"And both times were when a breeze came by?"

I rolled my eyes. "Sure. Technically, yes, it was windy yesterday. But did you not hear the part about the padlock and chain around the cemetery gates? About me knowing the front door was closed?"

"Your house is old, CC. The doors don't really close that well."

I bit my cheek to hold back my sigh. Of course he would take Gramps' side. The 'practical' side. But I couldn't help but wonder if there was more to this. Coincidence or not, I wanted to find a reason.

"I'm shocked, Ezra," I said.

"Why?"

"You're usually the one that sees all sides to a story, that understands there's a meaning for everything. And you're dismissing this just that quick? Not like you." I clucked my tongue and waved my finger at him disappointingly.

He narrowed his eyes, thinking. "I have one question first."

My lips curled up in a smile. I *knew* he would come up with something.

Ezra leaned in close, lowering his voice. "Who do you think you are, Teen Witch?"

I frowned and pushed him away. "You're so funny," I said sarcastically. "And your references are old. I'd be more like... Sabrina."

"As in Melissa or Kiernan?"

I didn't even have to think about that one. "Melissa, duh. The down on her luck girl who always has bad things happen to her who randomly finds out that she's a witch and her aunts—wait. Wait just a second. Do I have aunts somewhere that are witches and haven't told me?" My eyes grew wide as I thought about what it would mean to have family members that were also witches. Was Gramps? Gramma? Mom? Mom didn't have any siblings that I knew of, but maybe they were hiding until I developed my powers and--

"My great great great great something or another grandma might have been a witch. Did I tell you that?" Ezra asked, interrupting my spiraling. "I've been researching and—"

The bell cut him off. I pursed my lips and shrugged. "Whatever. I'll see you later?" I asked as we approached our breaking point. Ezra went left, and I went right.

I didn't really care much about his great whatever grand-mother. This was here and now and the present. This was an issue I had to deal with right away.

There had to be some way to figure out how to recreate those moments from yesterday again.

Too bad I didn't have more time to think about it before my History teacher slammed my test upside down on my desk, giving me a *look* before continuing down the row.

I closed my eyes and set up a silent prayer to anyone that would listen. I needed a good grade on this test to keep a B average in class. Anything less, and I would drop down to a C and Gramps would have a fit.

Holding my breath, I flipped the paper over. A bright red C- greeted me from the top of the page. I groaned inwardly, slumping down in my chair. Then I yelped as some strands of hair got caught in the screws behind my head.

After ripping out my hair, I sat up again and stared at the red mark. If there only was a way to change this...

My hands clenched into fists at my side as I became more and more upset. Mostly at myself, but also at Mr. Wether. I knew half of the class probably got a C or worse, as many of the questions on the test we hadn't gone over in class.

Were they potentially in the textbook I conveniently forgot in my locker the night before the test? Maybe. But had we covered it in class, I would have known the answer. Maybe.

My hands tingled from being held so tight. I loosened them and shook them out.

Maybe there was extra credit I could do. Maybe there was—

I paused as my fingers rubbed against each other, trying to get rid of the static-y feeling. As they did, I snapped once.

If it worked on a door... Could it work on my grade?

I focused on the C- written at the top, and snapped once again. Nothing happened. So I snapped twice in a row.

Still nothing.

I raised my hand to snap three times, but only got through the first one when Mr. Wether cleared his throat.

"Class, I have to apologize. It looks like I had the wrong stack of papers in my hand. Those were the tests for my next period. Please pass them to the front and I'll return yours. I'm happy to say you all did spectacularly on this particular exam. Everyone got an A. Which... has never happened before..." Mr. Wether reached up and scratched at his head, like he was seeing the grades for the first time as well.

We *all* got A's? That couldn't be possible. Mr. Wether was one of the hardest teachers in the school. Barely anyone ever passed his class with straight A's.

Slowly, I stared down at my hand. Did I do that? Was the sudden change because of me?

The lightbulb in my brain went off. Maybe it wasn't snapping *once*. Maybe it was *twice*.

All I really wanted was to change *my* grade, though. Not the entire classes. But... I didn't see the harm in that happening. It was a happy little accident for everyone.

And if I could do that... What else could I do?

Could I make Denise's perfectly slicked back ponytail have just one strand of hair come loose?

What about changing my lunch so I had pizza every day instead of the soggy peanut butter and jelly Gramps made for me this morning?

Could I finally get back at Scott for cheating on me sophomore year?

I needed to start small. I couldn't go making a big bang or anything. Maybe I could give Scott some zits or a rash. Something only I would know was from me.

I stared at the back of Scott's head and snapped twice.

Nothing happened.

I frowned, thinking really hard about revenge on Scott, and snapped twice *again*.

"What are you doing?" Wyatt, who sat across the aisle from me, asked.

I glared and shushed him, but froze when I saw something that freaked me out. My brows shot up my forehead as I glanced another row over, catching sight of Scott's twin brother Eric staring at me.

His chin rested in his hand, but his eyes looked like a cartoon character, full of giant hearts and stars. A goofy expression settled on his face as his head tilted sideways slightly.

Blinking, I looked around, wondering if anyone else was seeing this. Eric had never given me the time of day before, even when I dated Scott. Eric was the varsity football captain and student body president. He was the epitome of high school royalty. The kind that would no doubt crash and burn the second we graduated, only to go on with life reliving his best moments of his high school years.

Tentatively, I glanced back at him, finding his hair slightly messed up as he ran his fingers through it. After he did, he waggled them in my direction. *Waggled*. I had never defined anything before in my life as a waggle, yet watching him shimmy his fingers up and down while holding his hand straight out in my direction was definitely a waggle. Then, he lifted the same fingers to his mouth and blew me a kiss.

A *kiss*? Did he really just blow me a kiss from across the room? Oh no. No, no, no. What was he doing now? He scribbled something on a piece of paper, wadded it up, then chucked it toward me, where it landed by my shoe. I stomped on it, but didn't pick it up.

I stole one more look at Eric, finding him still staring, unable to rip his gaze away from me. He waved again, not quite the same waggle, but a definite wave, and definitely for me.

I didn't wave back. I sat straight up, staring at the whiteboard across the room, watching as Mr. Wether finished handing the tests back and consulted his gradebook one more time.

I shoved my hands under my thighs.

That was enough snapping for one class.

CHAPTER 6

I couldn't wait until lunch. I had to talk to Ezra *now*.

When we crossed paths again, I grabbed his arm and dragged him into the nearest broom closet.

The irony didn't escape me.

"What is going on?" he yelped, rubbing at his arm. "Why are we in the closet and where's the light switch?"

"Watch," I whispered. I thought super, super hard about the light turning on. The tingle in my fingers returned, I snapped twice, and a second later, we were bathed in a soft yellow glow.

The first thing I saw was Ezra's mouth hanging open. He blinked, whether from the sudden brightness or disbelief.

"You found the light switch?" he whispered, but the inclination behind his tone said that wasn't what he was thinking.

I needed to show him. I shook out my hands, frowning when I realized the tingling sensation was disappearing, and thought about turning the light off. Quickly, I snapped twice, but nothing happened. There was no insta-darkness like it had been the other way around.

I pouted. "So it doesn't work every time. And it definitely doesn't always work like I want it to, but did you *see* that? I turned the light on!"

Ezra stared at me, his mouth slowly closing. "Um, CC, I hate to break it to you, but the switch is right—"

He paused, though, when he saw the switch on the wall. It was still in the *off* position. His whole face fell while I smirked, watching him glance between the switch, me, me, the switch, and back.

"You... it's... how... snap?"

"Snap *snap*," I clarified. I didn't dare do the motion, as I didn't know what would happen.

"I was *right*?" he exclaimed with a fist pump.

I placed my hands on my hips and stared him down. "Excuse me? What do you mean, *you* were right?"

"I said you were a witch! Look what you did!"

"You said Teen Witch. *Sarcastically*," I answered smugly, reminding him just who had it right.

"Tomato, tomahto. That's not the point."

"What is the point? Because I'm freaking out. The gate? The door? And guess what happened just now in class..." I told him about getting the grades changed. Not just mine, but everyone's. The more I spoke, the more his face paled.

"Also, I think Eric, you know, Scott's brother, might be in love with me now. He was acting... weird."

"So this is real. Like *real* real. You're actually doing things by snapping your fingers."

"Mhm. It's not foolproof—"

"You have a lot to learn. But..."

"But what?" I asked as he trailed off, still glancing not so subtly at the light switch.

"Who's going to teach you? Are you hiding a letter to a boarding school in Europe that I don't know about?"

I shoved him, not amused by his jokes. He was usually the serious one, the rational one who made plans, dug for details, and tried to make sense of everything in the most logical manner. He wasn't the jester who tried to play off the insane amount of freaking out going on in their mind by cracking jokes.

That was my job in our friendship. However, I was somehow oddly calm about the entire situation. It almost felt... normal. Which made no sense, considering up until today I would have sworn witches and the supernatural wasn't real. Did I believe in ghosts? Maybe. Having a dead relative sort of made you wish ghosts were real sometimes. Past that, though, was all a big 'eh' for me. I never thought strongly one way or the other, especially without proof.

But proof like this? Undeniable.

"Alright, alright. Man, now I'm really mad I bailed last night." I started to comment, but he continued. "Do it again."

I grinned, wanting to show off just as much as he wanted to see it. "I'm not exactly sure of what to do, though. I didn't remember thinking about the gate or the door. The light, yes. But so far everything else has been kind of happenstance."

"Happy happenstance. Now do it again!"

"Your wish is my command," I said, raising my hand. I paused, thought, then said, "Well, not really. I'm not a genie. Just a witch. I think. Or something. Anyway..."

I couldn't think of anything else to do but turn the lights off, so that's what I focused on.

Snap snap.

Nothing.

"Um..." Ezra mumbled, looking around as if trying to find something different. "What was supposed to happen?"

"Shh!" I insisted, squeezing my eyes shut and focusing even harder. I imagined the room cloaked in darkness.

Snap snap.

"CC?" Ezra whispered.

I cracked my eyes open, expecting to see nothing from the dark. Except, I saw Ezra, a worried look over his face shadowed in the light that had yet to turn off.

That's when I heard it. The screams. The hollers. The lockers slamming shut.

"Umm..." Ezra's eyes grew wide at the same time as mine. He reached for the door handle a split second before me, and when it opened...

It was chaos. Pure, utter chaos.

The light from the closet streamed into the otherwise dark hallway. People standing in front of the door shielded themselves from the sudden rays, as if they hadn't seen light in years. Others bumped into each other, unable to see where they were going. Girls shrieked, books dropped, and guys kept saying 'bro' every time they collided.

"What did you do?" Ezra uttered.

I shrugged. Honestly, rude that he immediately thought it was me, but I had also, so, fair. "You think I did this?"

He spun and gave me a sharp look that said, *I absolutely do.* My face fell. I didn't *mean* to kill the lights in the entire school.

The odd thing was, it was *only* the lights. The TVs that hung at the top of the walls at the end of the hallway, reminding us of the time and schedule were still on. Projectors in the classroom across the hall still flickered through slides.

"The question is, CC, can you *undo* it?" Ezra was almost seething now, like he was upset with me because I caused such an issue. Teachers roamed around, patting the lockers to try to find their way, while also trying to console students.

I wanted to giggle at the sight as more students made their way toward Ezra and me, facing the only light source outside of cell phone flashlights.

"*CC!*"

"Okay, okay, I'll try." I shook my hands out at my side and tried to focus.

"Don't screw it up."

"Harsh."

"Just get it done, CC!"

I rolled my eyes, then shut them, thinking and focusing hard on getting the lights back on. I flexed my fingers, stretching them, then curling them into a ball.

That's when I felt it. The tingle returned.

Without opening my eyes, I pictured the hallway bright with the fluorescent lights, then snapped twice.

More shrieks greeted me, plus the sighs of relief.

"That's... weird," Ezra said.

Finally, I peeked open one eye and looked. The lights were on. Everyone was excitedly chatting amongst themselves about the crazy power outage.

"What's weird? I did it! I think I'm getting the hang of this," I said, lifting my hand up to my face to inspect my nails like what I just did was no big deal. "The Addams family has nothing on me."

"I would laugh, but you haven't turned around."

My hand froze in front of my face. I crossed one purple Doc Martin boot clad foot over the other, then slowly spun, looking back at the closet.

Which was now completely dark.

I dropped my hand to my side, my shoulders falling, a frown on my lips. "Aw *man*," I groaned, disheartened that it hadn't worked perfectly. "Well, I'm still getting used to it. I'll do better each time."

Ezra stepped in front of me, placed his hands on my shoulders, and said, "You absolutely will not. Promise me, CC, you will not go around causing chaos until we figure all of this out."

Sneaking my hands behind my back, I crossed my fingers, then said, "I promise. No chaos."

He nodded, then took off down the hall toward his class.

I grinned after him, uncrossing my fingers and turning in the opposite direction.

It's not like I *meant* to cause chaos. But what's life without a little fun?

CHAPTER 7

*S*nap *snap* became my new mantra that I repeated in my head over and over. Sometimes, when I actually snapped. Sometimes when I *wanted* to, but held some restraint.

Ezra would have been proud of me.

Or, maybe not.

Because the blue hair that ended up on Sally's head wasn't supposed to be blue. It was supposed to be an adorable cinnamon-rusty red color. I still had no idea where I went wrong with that. She hadn't noticed before I dashed down the opposite hallway. I had no idea what sort of state she was in now.

The backpack that had been weighing Toby down, causing him to have to hunch forward, was just supposed to be lighter. Not literally lift him up in the air, hovering a good foot over the ground for about five seconds.

But a few things did go right.

When Ellie came into the bathroom sobbing, saying her boyfriend had just broken up with her for no reason, a quick *snap snap* made that all better. By the time I washed my hands and left the bathroom, Ellie and Steve were making out against the lockers across the hall.

I had patted myself on the back for that one.

And when Duncan muttered to himself next to me in class about not being able to find his pencil, another *snap snap* had his backpack full of pencils.

Maybe a bit *too* full, but that wasn't the problem. Now he wouldn't ever have to look for one again. He could use one a day and be set for... an entire year.

The one thing I didn't do was cause chaos. Ezra said not to cause chaos, like killing the lights in the entire school, and I didn't. Simple as that.

So when he texted and told me to meet him at the Night Owl Café after school, I had nothing but confidence and a smile on my face. I wouldn't even have to lie. There had been no chaos caused.

"We need to figure out what is going on, CC," he said as soon as he slid into the chair opposite me. I pushed his tepid hot chocolate across the table toward him. It wasn't cooled off because I had been waiting a while; it was just the way he liked it.

As for me, I took a sip of my double chocolate chip blended coffee, made with two extra shots and topped with a mountain of whipped cream and chocolate drizzle.

"How does that not give you a headache, toothache, and stomachache?" Ezra asked, lifting his cup to his lips.

I slurped loudly in response, but didn't bother answering that question. Instead, I focused on his other one. "What do you mean, *we* have to figure out what's going on?"

He stared at me over the rim of the mug, behind his glasses, with raised eyebrows. If he were to die tomorrow, that would be exactly the face in my mind for the rest of my life. I had seen it more times than I could count.

"We," he emphasized, "need to find out what is going on with this snap snappity thing of yours, why it goes wrong, how to make it go right, and what it has to do with my great great great—"

"Okay, okay, I get it. Sort of. Not sure what your great whatever grandma has to do with this," I held up my hands, pretending I was going to snap, "but whatever. Let's figure it out."

Ezra lunged over the table and wrapped his hands over mine, glancing around to see if anyone was watching. It wasn't suspicious... until he did that. Stopping someone from snapping wasn't odd on a normal basis, but no one else here knew *why* he was stopping me from snapping.

"CC, you need to be smart about this. I want you to be *safe*." His eyes softened as he stared at me, as if he really were worried. "First things first," he said. "How did you even realize it was a snap?"

Thinking back, I started to connect the dots. But it went further back than I thought. "The carnival! Music. The beat."

"Excuse me, what? Some context, please."

With a grimace, I told him all about the carnival, how I dumped the pool of water and how it was full again. "It couldn't have been Janet. It was *me*! I was snapping along to the music, trying to keep myself from dancing."

"And for that, we are thankful," Ezra said with a sly grin. I rolled my eyes at him and stuck my tongue out.

"Anyway," I continued, launching into the story about how it connected to the cemetery gate, the front door, and my grades, and how they all came with snaps. "It was by mistake, I guess."

He nodded, like it made a ton of sense, but I could tell he was still deep in thought over it all.

"Did your great whatever grandma do any of this? Snap, I mean? I didn't know it was a thing. I thought witches used wands or wiggled their nose or something."

Ezra huffed out the tiniest of laughs at that. "I'm not sure. I haven't really gotten that far into that part of the history. I was organizing a family tree for Mom when I stumbled across some rumors. But I put it aside because it seemed so far-fetched it wouldn't be worth my time."

I sat back in the chair, crossing one leg over the other, and stared at him smugly. "But now..."

His cheeks flushed. "But now, I guess it's worth my time."

I beamed. "Awww. You could just say you're doing it because you love me, you know," I teased.

His whole face turned beet red, and he choked on his hot chocolate, sending small spittles over the table. If I were closer, I would have thumped him on the back, but I refrained. There were enough people looking at him right now.

Although... a thought came over me. I scrunched my nose, really, desperately trying to tamp it down and not act on impulse.

But being impulsive was *so* my thing.

Snap snap.

My jaw dropped as our drinks tumbled to the ground, smashing upon impact, liquid spraying in every direction, including all over our legs and feet.

It was almost as if I had watched it in slow motion. As soon as the drinks hit, I immediately tried again, needing to reverse what had just happened.

Snap snap.

Nothing.

Snap snap.

Still nothing.

"Cecilia!" Ezra muttered, his teeth gritted as he stared at the mess. I lifted my gaze to his, panicked.

I had just made the table disappear.

"I was only trying to clean up your spit!" I exclaimed, but softly, so no one else heard.

But they probably did. Because everyone was staring. It was sort of hard hiding the fact that your table up and vanished from under you. Especially when your drinks were currently laying on the ground.

Ezra jumped to his feet first, swinging his bag over his shoulder, grabbing mine with one hand, and clamping onto my arm with his other. In a flash, he hauled me off my chair, to the door, and down the street before I could realize what was going on.

We were two blocks away before he let go and gave me back my backpack.

"What. Happened."

I sighed and ran my fingers through my now knotty hair. "I don't know."

"You snap snappitied and snapped the table away!"

I narrowed my eyes and crossed my arms over my chest. "If you know exactly what happened, then why did you even bother asking?"

Ezra reached up and rubbed the bridge of his nose under his glasses, something he only did when he was stressed.

"No, the question is *why* the table snapped away," he shot back, as if annoyed with my question.

My brows furrowed. Ezra never usually spoke to me like this. He was the calm, even-tempered one who thought through every scenario and calculated data and his emotions accordingly. So why was he lashing out?

Sure, I made a table disappear in the middle of a crowded and busy coffee shop. Obviously, that wasn't a *good* thing. I knew that. There were probably going to be questions, and no one, including me, would have answers.

But I was just getting the hang of these new powers. It would take time. If he couldn't be patient, then who would? Certainly not me.

"I thought I could clean it up…" I whispered, suddenly embarrassed at my actions. I had done it in good faith, but it ended up going sideways, and now Ezra was mad at me.

"You have to be able to *manage* all of this, CC! Before you go out in public and mess around! What if someone saw you? What if someone—"

"Whoa, whoa, whoa. First of all, who would assume an eighteen-year-old girl who snapped her fingers magically made a table disappear? Not me, that's who. Who would even assume that a snap would be connected to a vanishing table? No spells, no wand waving, no flourish or sparkles? Nope. No one."

Ezra's hands moved from the bridge of his nose to his temples. "Not the point, *CC*."

I stomped my foot. "Then what *is* the point, *Ezra*?" I said his name with an oomph of sass behind it.

"The point is that you need to learn to manage this before someone gets hurt."

My eyes widened and my jaw dropped. "Hurt? You think I would be so reckless to do something where someone would get hurt?"

The hesitation and silence said that he did. The sharp pang in my chest ached harder than it should have. While I wasn't exactly known to be the most careful person on the planet, I wasn't about to do something to purposefully hurt someone else, and Ezra should have known that.

"What I think we need to do—"

"Pardon *moi*, but what do you mean by 'I?' Don't you mean *me*?"

He sighed and finally dropped his hands from his face. "Of course. But—"

"Nope. Try again."

His shoulders sagged, and I knew the old Ezra was back. "CC, you have to admit, this could be dangerous."

"I admit."

"And you need someone to help you along the way."

"Find me a witch teacher and we'll talk." The smirk on my face was in jest, but he didn't return it. "Or do you want to send me away to a boarding school in a castle on the edge of a cliff overlooking a giant lake?"

He shook his head, not even acknowledging that I had built on top of the joke he made before. Whatever. He could be pissy if he wanted to be.

"That's the problem, actually. We don't know anyone else who could help you. What do we do, walk around watching everyone's hands and seeing if they snap? Every time someone snaps, do we watch out for something weird happening?"

I pursed my lips and thought. It wasn't a *bad* idea, but definitely sounded stalkerish and time consuming. "So what do I do?" I made sure to emphasize the 'I,' just to remind him who really was behind all of this.

Ezra tilted his head side to side, cracking his neck, which usually drove me insane, but I barely noticed it now. Then, he took off down the street, toward our houses. I followed along, falling in step with him quickly, despite the height difference.

"I think we need to find what the commonality is between all the times that work," he said matter-of-factly.

I nodded. "That's easy. The tingle."

"The tingle? There's a tingle? Why haven't you mentioned a tingle? Where is the tingle? What is the tingle? How does the tingle—"

"You've said tingle so many times now that it's become icky and also doesn't even sound like a real word anymore," I interrupted. "Tingle. *Tingle.* Tingle." The more I said the word, the odder it sounded.

"CC, focus, please. For just another minute."

I jerked out of my thoughts. "Oh, yeah. The tingle." I cringed. "I can't be sure it's been every time, because sometimes the snap comes faster than my brain thinks, but mostly, before I snap, there's a tingle in my hand. Like when your foot falls asleep or you get an electric shock or you hit your funny bone and—"

"Just in that one hand?"

"In whatever hand I snap with, usually my right, yeah."

"So the tingle is the magic," he stated, as if he knew all the answers. Truthfully, he probably did and would continue to know more than me, even though I was the one experiencing everything.

I frowned, pondering, as I kicked a rock on the sidewalk. "The tingle is the magic? That seems... weird. What I'm more confused about is why it hasn't shown up before *now*. Why on Halloween?"

Ezra shot me a look and raised his brows. He couldn't raise just one like I could. But then again, I could flare my nostrils on command and he couldn't either. One time, when I had just gotten a cavity filled and the left side of my face was numb, I tried flaring my nostrils and only the right one worked and he thought it was so funny he accidentally spat his soda out of his mouth and his nose, drenching me in the process.

I never flared them for him again. On purpose, that was.

"Halloween, witches, paranormal activity, all that, I get it. But why me? Why *now*? Why not, like, on my eighteenth birthday or something?"

Ezra scratched his head. I knew I had him. They were legit questions, and he didn't have an answer. Yet.

"I'll do some research," he said as we reached the walkway to his house.

"On your great whatever grandmother?" I asked, as that seemed to be at least a loose connection. If his ancestor was really a witch and it wasn't just a rumor, maybe it could be a jumping off point to think about me, too.

"Starting there, yeah. See you tomorrow?" He gave me a half smile, almost an apologetic one, which I accepted with a grin of my own.

"See you tomorrow."

He turned and walked toward his house. As he stood in the open doorway, he called out, "No funny business! I mean it!"

I waved, but pretended I couldn't hear him before jogging the last few yards to my own house. I knew he would be shaking his head before ducking inside, and that made me laugh.

Funny business. Nothing, and everything, about this situation was funny.

CHAPTER 8

L ike a good girl, I did as Ezra asked. There was no funny business last night. Mainly because I was up late studying and doing homework like the good student I should have been. I had vowed to myself *not* to change my grades again, even though it had been for the benefit of the entire class.

But... doing that too much would definitely bring up some red flags and cause notice by the teacher. Like Ezra implied, I had to stay under the radar. At least for now. Until I could control things.

That was my motto: until I could control things. Once I could do that, it was open season, baby. At least, maybe. Was I breaking some sort of magical law? Would someone throw me into witch jail?

Thinking of that on the way to school brought up another question—if this suddenly appeared in my life, did anyone else know? Could there be a council somewhere that had been alerted? Would they come try to find me and take me away and...

Before I could continue that train of thought, Ezra caught up to me. His hair was knotty, his jeans rumpled, and I was almost certain he had on the same shirt as yesterday. Even his glasses were slightly askew on his nose, and a pillow crease settled on his right cheek.

"Um... are you okay?" I asked, softly, just in case he had a headache from no sleep.

He nodded, his glasses slipping down his nose as he did. "Yeah. Just stayed up all night researching."

"Define *all night*."

"What time is it now?"

I checked the clock on my phone. "Seven forty-two."

"Then I got exactly two hours and thirty-three minutes of sleep," he shot back quickly. I didn't even know how he did the math that fast. I was still trying to calculate the hour in my head.

"You were up until..." I gave up and rounded. "Until five in the morning? How much could you possibly have found?"

"More than you think," he answered, then stretched his hands over his head and let out a large, loud yawn. His shirt lifted over his torso, exposing his abdomen. It wasn't a washboard like some of the jocks, but it wasn't bad to look at either. "Answer me this first—why do you live with your grandpa?"

My whole face scrunched up. He knew this answer already. "Um, why?"

"Just humor me."

"Because my mom left me on their doorstep the day I was born, no one knew who my dad was, and then Gramma died a few years after that." My tone was rather flat. It wasn't a subject I particularly enjoyed talking about.

"Right. I knew that." *Duh.* "But that's exactly what I wanted to hear."

"Please do me a favor and get to the point. This hasn't kicked in yet." I lifted the coffee mug in my hand to show him the caffeine juice I had only gotten halfway through. It was one of my favorite mugs. Well, they were all my favorites. But this one was in the shape of a skull and I drank out of its empty brain cavity.

"I don't think your mom left."

My hand jerked at that bomb drop, so much so that some of the hot liquid splashed out and onto my hand. "Ah! Crap, ouch, ouch."

Ezra expertly grabbed the mug out of my hand, then used the hem of his shirt to wipe at my hands. He was always cleaning up my messes or fixing me up when I got hurt by being clumsy. A second later, he carefully handed me back the mug, to the non-injured hand this time.

"Why don't you have some sort of travel mug? Or something with a lid?"

I shrugged. "Because I love my mugs."

"You collect them," he said, as if there was a difference. "Why can't you collect a travel mug?"

"Doesn't fit the aesthetic. And stop trying to change the subject. You can't just drop a bomb like you don't think my mom left and then move away from it that fast. What do you mean you don't think she left? You think she's... you think she's dead?"

I stopped on the sidewalk as the realization of what he meant hit me. Did he find something I didn't know about? Was Gramps hiding this from me all these years?

Gramps said at first, Mom would send a postcard from wherever she was. She hightailed it to New York, then another came from London, then some tiny town in Spain. After about six months, they stopped, and he hadn't gotten one since.

I knew for a fact he had kept them, though, in the back of the junk drawer in the kitchen, covered by random utensils and screwdrivers and old magnets. I found them when I was seven, but he didn't explain anything about them. That was also around the time he started making up stories about her disappearance in my life.

"What?" Ezra said, stepping in front of me. "No! Oh geez, CC, I didn't mean it like that!" He pulled at his dark-brown hair, in desperate need of a haircut, and frowned. "No, I don't think she's dead. Nothing I found makes me think that. I'm sorry if it came out wrong. I just meant... I don't think she *left*."

I cocked my head to the side, pushing away the negative thoughts, and was now thoroughly confused. "Huh?"

We started walking again, side by side, keeping our voices low even though there was no one around us. "Here's what I found. My great great great—"

"Great whatever," I interrupted, not wanting to hear him count the greats.

"Great whatever grandmother really was a witch. According to rumors, but from what I've found, rumors seem substantial. And after searching for a good while, I think your ancestors were, too. They were all part of a circle—"

"You mean coven." I didn't know much about witches, but I was pretty sure a group of them was called a coven, with all of them standing around a giant caldron, stirring a bubbly, smoky green liquid. Come to think of it, where did one acquire such a large cauldron? I highly doubted any local retailer had such an item.

"No, I mean circle. It's what they called their groupings. Now, most of the circles were within the same family, with branches out as families expanded. It looked like it was rare for a non-family member to be a part, or for someone to leave their family circle."

"Hmm." I didn't know what to think about that, or what it had to do with his great whatever grandma, or my own ancestors. But I was sure he would tell me soon enough.

"Here's the crazy thing," Ezra continued.

"Just now we're getting to the 'crazy thing?' As if everything before today was normal?" I teased, but he paid me no attention. It was hard to get him to focus on other things if he was on a roll, so I shut my mouth and let him talk.

"My great *whatever* grandma's brother was married to someone in *your* family's circle."

That got me to stop again. "Say what?"

He smiled and pushed his glasses up. His grin highlighted his pillow crease. "Yup. The brother married someone named Sonya. But the odd thing is, I couldn't find anything else on her or her original circle. She just appeared in my family tree. Which would be fine, but only witches appeared in the circle records. It wasn't until I started looking for *your* family circle that the dots connected."

"What does that mean? You're saying a few hundred years ago—"

"Two hundred and sixty-three."

"My ancestor was in the same family circle as yours?"

"Yes, but it's not what you think it is. I think she *left* your family circle to go to what I guess would be my family circle after that, as she married someone in my family."

"But you said no one really left their own family circles." None of this was making sense, and we were almost at school now. He needed to hurry up and get straight to the matter. Why would marrying someone make her leave her family? Why couldn't she stay with her family and still be married to this guy, especially if it seemed like women held all the power?

"True. *Almost* no one. Sonya was different. After she left your family circle, I tried to go look and see what happened. But I couldn't find anything. It was like she joined my circle and disappeared. There's no more documentation of her after the marriage."

I let out a big breath. "Okay. Well, I don't know what any of this means. One question, though—does that mean we're related?"

Ezra held up a finger and thought. "I don't *think* so. Even if we were both from this Sonya girl, it would be like a billion times removed by now. So if I had to say, I'll go with no." Ezra mumbled something under his breath, but I didn't catch it. Something about being thankful. The tips of his ears burned red, but I ignored it for now.

"Right. So Sonya got married, left my circle, went to your circle, and then... what? She disappeared? Your circle obviously survived. And mine? I'm guessing you found something because you traced me back to her."

His eyes snapped up to mine. "That... is all sort of complicated. But the reason I found out she was connected to you was because your middle name is her last name."

"It's a family name."

Ezra nodded, as he already knew that. Potentia wasn't a common name for anyone, anywhere, but I shared it with my mom and grandmother.

"I noticed that right away. It was the only thing I could find about Sonya, before she joined my circle. Sonya Potentia became Sonya Furtado, and then there was nothing else about her."

I bit the inside of my cheek, trying to process all this information. Ezra and I were descendants of witches. A witch from my family married into his.

"What about the rest of my family? What happened to them?"

We were still standing on the walkway to the front doors of school now with students walking around us as we ignored them all. "That's the weird thing. I was able to eventually find the family Sonya came from because of the name. I followed the path down, and... your circle just... *ends*. With your mom..."

I blinked. Then blinked again. Then spun in a circle, waved my hands in front of Ezra's face, and pinched myself on the arm. "But... I'm pretty sure I exist."

He nodded slowly. "That you do."

"Am I a ghost? Is this like some sort of ghost limbo? That makes sense. Make limbo for teenagers a public high school. That's torture enough. Can you imagine—"

"You aren't a ghost, CC," Ezra said, exasperated by now.

"Maybe you're a ghost, too. Maybe we're all ghosts." I spread my arm out wide, gesturing to the high school in front of me. "Maybe this whole town is a ghost town!"

Ezra shook his head. "It's not a ghost town, CC. You are not a ghost. I am not a ghost. You exist. Just not in your family circle. By everything I can find, your circle just... ends. Like it's gone. It doesn't exist. Your mom and grandma were the last two named. Everyone else on the list just... stops. There isn't a single person in your mom's generation, either. She was literally the last."

"You keep saying girl names," I said after the lightbulb went off. I would figure out what he meant by the circle ended later. And the fact that both my mother and grandmother were witches, yet no one ever told me. Not even Gramps. "Why is it only girls?"

Ezra jumped to the side as another student rushed past him, apparently eager to get into the school as fast as possible. We climbed the stairs that lead to the front doors, then he answered me.

"I'm not sure. It looks like only the women are... *you know*," he said in a hushed whisper, as there were lots of people around now.

"What about the guys?"

"I haven't figured that out yet. I think they played a role, but I don't know what it was. That's tonight's rabbit hole."

We reached the hallway intersection where we normally separated, but I had one more thought.

"Ezra... if there are... *you knows* around... what about other things? Like vampires or aliens?" I was so serious, but I could tell he didn't believe me. There could be a whole world out there that I didn't know about, an entirely different universe hidden from us. If witches were real, why not other paranormal beings? Did the gargoyles on top of the bank come alive at night? Did bats turn into vampires when we weren't looking? Maybe the school had ghosts haunting the halls and we just couldn't see them.

"Well," he replied, schooling his face to pretend he was giving this actual thought, "we haven't explored space enough to exclude aliens."

My eyes lit up at the possibility. "And vampires?"

Ezra leaned in close and I started bouncing on my toes. "There's lots of documentation in history about vampires, mainly in fictional stories. But we all know fiction is derived from reality at some point..."

CHAPTER 9

This time, the tingles found me. Ezra couldn't even complain, because it technically wasn't my fault.

First, my right hand became tingly, like pins and needles. It was slightly different from the other times, but in the same sense. Then, it almost felt like it went numb. I grew concerned as class went on, my panic rising after the bell rang.

As I walked down the hallway, I shook it out a little, trying to get it to go away, but it didn't.

So I did the only thing I could think of doing. I snapped.

Snap snap.

Turned out, that was probably a bad idea because I had no intention behind the snap and therefore, it went rogue. However, in my mind it had been the right thing to do, because I figured if my hand became tingly, then maybe there was some sort of inner witch who knew what was going on and what would happen.

As my random bad luck would have it, the inner witch was thirsty. The water bottle filling fountain across the hallway exploded, sending sprays of water *everywhere*.

It soaked the head football coach, who stood outside his health and wellness classroom talking to the star quarterback. Star was a bit much, but wasn't every high school quarterback described as a star? Our team had only won two games out of ten so far this season, but whatever.

They were drenched head to toe. The papers in Coach's hand fell to the ground in a wet heap as the QB stood frozen to the spot, his mouth agape, streams of water dripping from his raised hands.

The water also shot out to the left, getting the QB's cheerleader girlfriend straight in the face. Her mascara streaked down her cheeks and her hair plastered to her ears.

The last victims were, unfortunately, my friends, standing across the hall from the explosion, waiting for me to join them. Thankfully, I was about ten feet from the spray zone and stayed dry, but they didn't.

It took a full minute for the sprays to turn into trickles, then shut off. Everyone in the hallway stood quietly, watching in horror at the scene in front of them.

If Ezra was here, he would take my hand and run me out of sight, like he did at the coffee shop. But I couldn't think of anyone who would assume what happened was *my* fault. Just like the lights the other day.

I waited until other people began moving before heading towards my now wet friends. Right before I made it, though, a shiver went up my spine, and a feeling like someone was watching me came over me.

Pausing, I spun around and looked to see if someone was behind me. There were people, of course, but none with their attention on me. Same to my right—the coach and his star were currently trying to make sense of what happened and failing.

But as I looked over Miranda's soggy shoulder, I found someone. Someone I didn't recognize. A tall kid, with the darkest hair I had ever seen, and a white streak from his eye to behind his ear.

A teenager with a white streak of hair? That I would have noticed before.

But as soon as I saw him, he disappeared, dashing down the opposite corridor. I turned my attention to my damp friends.

"Um, so that happened," I said nervously. What else was I supposed to say? *Sorry I snapped and broke the water fountain and it sprayed like a geyser all over the hallway?* Yeah, that wasn't happening.

Miranda stared at me, tiny droplets clinging to her dark lashes. She didn't wear mascara because she already had the most gorgeous natural eyelashes any woman had ever seen. "Yup. That happened. What is going on at this school? First the random power outage, now this?"

"I mean, the building itself is like a hundred years old," Matt replied. He wasn't wrong, but the district did a huge overhaul only a few years ago, replacing the roof, windows, lighting, electrical and a ton of other things while we were off on break.

"Maybe the renovations had an expiration date," I offered with a shrug.

Miranda shook her head, bits of water flying in all directions. I ducked, and she laughed. "Sorry. I guess now... Actually I don't know what to do. Coach," she yelled across the hall, "do I have permission to go home?"

Coach whipped his head toward her. "If you think this will get you out of your quiz today, you're wrong, Miss Santiago. Go change into your P.E. clothes, stat."

Miranda and Matt both groaned. I grimaced, emphasizing with them. No one wanted to wear their P.E. clothes all day. It was like social suicide.

"Maybe you can call your mom to bring you some extra stuff? I might have a sweater in my gym locker..." Miranda's eyes widened at the thought. She could pull off the sweater and black gym shorts combo.

Matt was on his own. I wouldn't have anything to fit his massive, broad shoulders and wide hips. There was a reason he played linebacker. I was sure it was his size, because it wasn't his personality. I had a feeling after every hit, or block, or whatever they called it, he helped pick the person up and apologized to him profusely.

After I rattled off my locker combo to Miranda, she bolted down the hallway, Matt following after her, headed to the guy's locker room.

I turned to go to class, careful not to slip on the wet linoleum floors. The last thing I needed was to fall and accidentally snap my fingers again.

I didn't even mean to do it this time. That darn tingle started going crazy, to the point where it almost hurt. The only way I thought I could get it to stop was to snap.

Note to self: when performing magic, wait for the tingle, have a *clear* thought in your head, then snap. Under no circumstance do you snap before the tingle or without a plan.

That was going to be a problem, and I already knew it. I wasn't one to think before I jumped, so thinking before snapping could be problematic as well.

I let out a deep sigh, knowing Ezra would be so mad at me thinking I had gone around causing chaos. Even if it wasn't really my fault. It was my *magic's* fault. I didn't ask for my hand to start tingling so badly it felt like I was being stabbed.

I also wondered what that could mean. *Why* did it randomly go off when it had never done that before? Why then? Was it because I hadn't used it in a while? Did magic store up and you had to get rid of some before you exploded?

Maybe it was—*oof*.

A second later, I somehow ended up on my butt, the air almost knocked out of my lungs, my head rattling a little bit.

It wasn't so bad that I saw stars, like that one time I jumped down from a tree branch, misjudged the height, and crash landed, smashing my head into the dirt. That was the day I knew the bird who saw the stars circling his head every time he fell in the cartoons was based on reality.

While there were no stars, there was a prickling sensation flowing through me. It wasn't the same as the tingling in my hands, but similar. It wasn't goosebumps; this felt deeper somehow, like an internal shiver that traveled from my spine, trickling up my neck, into my head, and down into my arms until it spread everywhere.

It was the second time I felt it today, the first being—

Oh. Well, that was spot on.

As I looked up, I found the culprit behind my fall. A giant of a person, tall and built, but not overly muscular. More like I could tell there were defined muscles under his clothes, but nothing clung to him tight enough for me to know exactly how many abs he had.

My gaze traveled from his black shoes, up his jeans, to his plain V-neck black t-shirt, to his chiseled cheekbones and finally, his pushed back black hair...

...with a white streak along the side.

It was the same kid from a few minutes ago. And I was getting massive 'stay away' vibes from him. I wasn't sure what about him creeped me out, but I was both terrified and intrigued.

Who was he? When did he get here? And what was he doing in front of *my* locker?

"Sorry," he finally said. "Though you actually ran into *me*."

An accent. Of course tall, dark, and handsome had an English accent. Every girl in this school would be all over him in a hot minute. Except for me. Besides giving me a weird feeling in my gut, the fact that he hadn't even tried to stop me from falling left me with little desire to do anything with him.

I groaned, rubbing the back of my head even though I didn't hit it on the ground.

He cleared his throat, and that was when I realized he had held his hand out to help me up. Despite all the nerves in my arm begging me not to accept, I did, and he lifted me to my feet with ease.

"I'm Xavier," he said, still holding my hand. That's when he flashed me the brightest grin I had ever witnessed in my life. His teeth were fantastic, a shade of white that would make dentists weep with joy, and all perfectly straight, likely the work of a fantastic orthodontist.

"Um, Cecilia," I answered, my mind still stuck trying to figure out if anyone had seen this little show. Did they think I was trying to get his attention? No doubt many other girls would do the same soon. Xavier was new, hot, and had an accent. Girls were going to throw themselves at his feet.

Which was *not* what I was doing.

It wasn't really my fault, though. No one had the locker next to mine for three years now. Suddenly, he comes along, and I'm just supposed to know the human equivalent of a cement wall would block my locker? Literally, there was no bounce back with this guy; he was as solid as one could be.

Maybe that was my turn off—he must have been a gym bro. I couldn't stand guys who spent every waking moment grunting in a stinky, sweaty room while looking at themselves in a mirror.

"Cecilia? *You're* Cecilia?" He said it as if it were impossible, like I must have had my own name wrong.

Did I? Maybe I did hit my head and my name wasn't Cecilia—wait. No. I definitely was Cecilia. Why was he looking at me like I was mistaken?

I blinked. Then blinked again while shaking my head. A long lock of hair fell into my face, catching on my lip gloss when I tried to open my mouth.

And then, my whole body went into overdrive. Not from the hair. But from Xavier, standing in front of me, staring at me like I was about to pass out.

He reached out and put both hands on my upper arms to steady me. Right as his last finger curled around my bicep, the tingles mixed with the shivers from my head to my toes.

And I blacked out.

CHAPTER 10

"CC? Cecilia? Come on, CC, this isn't funny, you have to wake up."

The voice floating around me seemed familiar, but I couldn't place it. Not until I rubbed at my eyes and found a massive face with giant glasses staring down at me from above.

"Ahh!" I screamed, rolling to the side to get away from the person. But as I did, I subsequently rolled myself *out* of the cot I was lying on and onto the floor.

"Ow! Ah! Ow!" I alternated between being freaked out and in pain.

I heard someone sigh behind me. Turning to look over my shoulder, I found the monster with the glasses to be Ezra, currently rubbing at the bridge of his nose. "Seriously, CC? What am I supposed to tell Nurse Paige? She's going to think I pushed you or something."

Once my heart rate dropped, I sat up, resting my arms on my knees, but didn't move to stand just yet. "Nah. She knows me better than that. She'll know I fell out of bed. Speaking of bed... *why* am I on Nurse Paige's cot?"

I tried to think back to the last thing I could remember, but it came up a bit fuzzy. There was the water fountain... Miranda and Matt... then... nothing.

Did I slip in a puddle? That had to be it. I must have been hurrying past and slid on the wet floor and knocked myself out or something. It would be so typical of me.

"Oh no!" I gasped, bringing my hands to my face. "You found out?" I peeked through my fingers, looking at Ezra.

He frowned, his brows pulling in with confusion. "Found out what?"

"The water!"

"What water?"

"In the hall? The fountain exploding? The massive amount of water that drenched everyone in a ten foot radius that I must have stepped in and super ungracefully barreled my way to the floor, knocking myself unconscious?" I dropped my hands, staring at him openly, wondering just how much he knew and how much I just gave away.

His eyes widened behind his frames. He leaned in and spoke in a hushed whisper. "A water fountain *exploded*? What did you do?"

I rolled my eyes. Of course he would blame me first. This little party trick was getting old, especially since I just told him I probably put myself into a quick coma from it. "First of all, it wasn't my fault." His face relaxed. "Not *really* my fault. Sort of my fault, but also not."

Now he looked more confused than before. "Make that make sense, CC, before my head explodes."

"See now *that* wouldn't be my fault!"

"CC!"

"Fine, fine. Wait," I paused, a thought appearing light bulb style in my mind. "If you didn't know about the water, how did you know I was here? And how long have I been here?"

Ezra shrugged. "I was walking by after sixth period and saw you laying here through the window. Gramps is on the way, Nurse Paige said."

That got me to my feet. "*Sixth* period? Ezra, the water was like," I checked my phone, "three hours ago! Are you saying I've been passed out for three hours?"

He shrugged again. "I'm saying *I don't know, CC*, because I just saw you here, like, two minutes ago. Are *you* saying you've been here for three hours?"

The look on my face must have worried him just as much as I was worried on the inside, because he also leapt to his feet. "Wait, if you've been here for three hours, why hasn't your gramps come to get you yet?"

We stared at each other for a moment, before Ezra pushed back the curtain. "Nurse Paige! How long has Cecilia been in your office?"

She peeked her head around from inside the closet-sized room with a one-person desk and said, "About ten minutes, dear. Not that long before you got here. Is she up? How is she doing? She looked so tired."

"Who brought her in?" Ezra asked, ignoring her questions.

Nurse Paige opened her mouth to answer, but then stopped and scratched her head. "I... I can't remember."

I grabbed Ezra's hand and pulled him back toward the cot. "I need to get out of here. *Now*."

He nodded. "Text your gramps. Tell him you're fine and I'm taking you home."

"He won't let me walk home if he was called here because I passed out, Ezra."

"Well, what do you want me to do?" Ezra threw his hands in the air. "I can't magically make a car appear—"

A slow, sly smile stretched across my face as he abruptly stopped talking.

"No. CC, *absolutely not*. You can't even clean up a mess without making a table disappear! You cannot conjure a car out of thin air!"

I frowned. He was right. It would have been awesome to try, though, but deep inside I knew it could end in disaster.

"Text him and tell him Miranda is driving you back," Ezra said, poking his head around the curtain. "That you're going to my place to rest. Nurse Paige said you looked tired, remember?

Maybe you came in because you needed a nap and not because you passed out. Honestly, I have *no idea what is happening*."

His plan made sense. Ezra's mom was a holistic healer of sorts. I never quite understood when Ezra explained it, but it had a lot to do with tinctures and herbal salves and such. Whatever it was, she was good at it, because Ezra and Fisher were rarely sick.

"He'll buy that," I said, my fingers flying over my phone. Somehow that had made it to the nurse with me, along with my bag. After I shot off the message, I scanned inside my bag, finding nothing I would have needed for the past three hours. It was like my life stopped right at the water explosion.

"Okay, the coast is clear. Let's blow this popsicle stand," Ezra whispered.

I paused before zipping up my bag. There was one thing gone.

My headphones.

I liked the big ones, the ones that shut out the entire world and let me practically live in the music. Mine collapsed slightly, the earpieces folding in. I kept them in a velvet pouch I found in the spare bedroom one day, just to keep them safe from all the other junk in my backpack.

"Ezra... my headphones are missing."

"That's nice. We have to go."

I followed his lead, swinging my backpack over my shoulder and crouching behind him to the door. We darted out of the nurse's office without being seen. When we got to the side exit, I focused on the alarm system attached to it, felt the now familiar tingle in my fingers, then *snap snapped*.

I didn't have time to marvel at the fact that it worked before Ezra pulled me out, the door slamming behind us.

Once we were clear of the school, I looked at Ezra, my heart pounding.

"What is it? What's wrong? Is it your head? Can you walk? Are you okay?"

I waved him off. "I'm fine. Oddly enough, I feel completely fine. Nothing aches, nothing hurts." That thought worried me for a second. If I had fallen hard enough to be out for three hours, shouldn't my head hurt? "But Ez... you've never skipped school before. Ever."

He stopped for a second, looking behind him. "That's true. Guess there's a first time for everything."

"Are you sure? You can go back. I can make it home. Really, I feel perfectly fine. Maybe I should actually go back to class." We had already reached the cemetery a few blocks away, but were still close enough. I turned to walk away when a hand on my arm stopped me.

My entire world went dark for a moment, my vision clouding over, blackness replacing the sunshine. There was something there... but I couldn't quite see. Was it a person? An animal? Where was I? It looked... It looked like small tables surrounded me.

No, it wasn't quite tables. They were too small and didn't have flat tops. These had more of flat sides...

"CC? Cecilia, what are you doing?"

I jolted back to reality, the cloudiness disappearing in an instant. The sun became almost too bright. I shielded my eyes, looking down at the sidewalk.

Sidewalk. Shoes. Jeans. Sweater.

Sweater.

"Ezra... if I slipped in the water, why aren't my clothes wet?"

"Cecilia, where did you go just now? You were completely zoned out. I called your name, and you didn't answer. I almost snapped my fingers in front of your face, but I got too scared for that."

A wave of calm washed over me at that. It wasn't meant to be a joke, but it still made me laugh. "Oh, I'd *love* to see you do a little snappity snap and see what happens."

Ezra's face went about as pale as it could before his cheeks flushed once more. "Seriously, are you okay?"

"Yeah... it was weird." I wanted to explain what I had seen, but the more I tried to figure out words, the more it sounded like I made the whole thing up. "Anyway. Why aren't my clothes wet? There was so much water on the floor, I should have gotten soaked."

A thoughtful look crossed his face as we continued to walk. Ezra took my bag off my shoulder, hoisting it over his. "I'm not sure. I mean, maybe there wasn't a lot of water in the spot you slipped and it's since dried?"

Sometimes I hated when he used logic to give sensible answers. If I had been out for three hours, then sure, my clothes could have dried in that time. It wasn't the answer I was looking for. Probably because I wasn't asking the question I needed.

"Ezra," I started again, "where was I for three hours? The last thing I remember is the water fountain explosion, but you said it was sixth period when you saw me."

"Yeah."

"So... I'm missing *three hours*." I tried to put some emphasis on it, because it didn't seem like a big deal to him.

He was silent for a few more moments as we walked, only a couple of houses away from his now. "Well... maybe it's your brain protecting you or something. Maybe you didn't slip in the water like you think? Nurse Paige said you had only been there for about ten minutes before I got there."

"What else could have happened? And who brought me to the nurse?"

Once again, he didn't answer right away. Either he was thinking or he was coming up with something else to tell me, which would only placate me.

"I should have asked," he muttered under his breath. He was mad with himself for not investigating a situation he didn't know needed investigating?

"This whole thing is weird," I stated as we turned up his walkway. "Something is off, but I don't know what."

If I had to bet, that something had to do with whatever I saw in that darkness.

Chapter 11

E zra fixed us both a snack and grabbed some sodas while I waited in the living room. Every time I turned sharply, I thought my head would hurt. By all means, it *should* hurt.

But then again, I *should* have been able to account for three missing hours.

"Okay, so the last thing you remember is the water fountain. Why don't you tell me what happened?" Ezra said after he returned, putting an already sweating glass of icy cold soda in my hands.

I clung to it, not caring that it was dripping onto my jeans, and explained about the tingling. "It was like... like when your foot falls asleep and takes too long to wake up. You try everything—stomping, shaking, slapping it, even pinching and it just doesn't wake up."

"And you thought snapping would make it go away?" he said, lifting his glass to his mouth and taking a soundless sip.

I was more of a gulper, especially with my favorite drinks. But I hadn't even taken a taste yet. "Well, yeah. I mean, it goes away every other time I snap, so why not this time?"

"So what went wrong?"

My brows raised as I lifted a finger into the air. "Aha! See, here's what I've come up with—" I paused, my head suddenly *pounding*. "I... I snapped and... the water fountain exploded because... because... I wasn't... wasn't thinking... owwww."

I put the glass down on the table and clutched at my forehead. Was this the hurting that should have come earlier? Why was it *killing* me?

"CC? Are you okay?" The question had been parroted so many times, it was about to lose meaning.

But right now, I needed it. "Medicine. Need medicine." I needed something to get rid of this pounding. The more I thought about why the water fountain blew up, the more it hurt.

I knew I had caused it. I knew the tingles in my hands made me snap, and then it exploded. What I couldn't figure out was *why* or how the two were connected. Whenever I tried to connect the dots, my brain felt like it was the fountain, ready to explode out of my skull.

Ezra hurried out of the room just as the sides of my vision became fuzzy. A migraine. That's what was happening.

I didn't get them often, only about once a year or so, but they were usually unexpected like this. And one of the only things that helped was actually Ezra's mother's salves.

He was back before another wave hit, already having expected what was going on. He knew me better than I knew myself, apparently.

I didn't even have to move. He went into autopilot, rubbing the salve onto my temples, laying me down, and lifting my feet. I grabbed the nearest pillow and put it over my face, blocking any light that came from the windows.

A few minutes later, the migraine subsided enough that I could talk. I stayed under the pillow, my feet on Ezra's lap.

"Tell me more about your research," I said, hoping I could just lie here and listen to him speak.

"Oh, now that you mention it," he started, squeezing my leg, "I found something really weird."

"My family tree or yours?"

"Mine."

"Have you spoken with your mom about what you found? Did she have any insight?"

"Not yet, and here's why—she's not on the list. The list suddenly stops like forty years ago or so."

I wanted to sit up and see if he was joking or not, but I thought better about it. Another question crossed my mind, though.

"Do you think if I snap, my headache will disappear?"

Ezra's grip on my ankle tightened. "Don't you even think about it. I don't need to watch your entire head vanish like the table!"

I grinned from under the pillow, even though he couldn't see me. "Okay, okay, fine. Back to your mom. She's not on the list?"

"Nope."

"My mom was on a list. But not me."

"Yep."

"What does that all mean? Why does your family circle just suddenly stop and mine goes an extra generation or two?"

I could feel him shrug from next to me. "I don't know. I'll do some more research tonight and see what else I can find."

"As long as you don't stay up until five in the morning again," I teased. "You need your sleep or you'll start hallucinating."

The smile on his face was evident in his voice. "About what, witches and vampires and aliens?"

A loud crash came from the hallway behind us just then. I chucked the pillow off my face and bolted upright, right as Ezra pushed my legs off of his lap and jumped to his feet.

"Mom! You're home!"

Leaning over the back of the couch, I saw a grocery bag full of boxes for the pantry had fallen to the floor. Ezra's mom's face was white, as if she had seen a ghost.

"What did you say?" she asked quietly, but she wasn't looking at Ezra. She was staring straight at me.

"I said you're home? I didn't realize you'd be here so early," Ezra repeated.

"No before then."

He bent down and picked up the boxes, stacking them neatly into the reusable bag. "Oh, witches, vampires, and aliens? It was a joke CC had from Halloween the other day. Remember, she was a basic witch again?"

His mom's gaze was still on me, so I nodded emphatically. "Yup. That's me, always the witch for Halloween. Can't go wrong with a classic, right Mrs. Fallere?"

Her head followed mine, bobbing up and down for a few seconds, until she seemed to come through. Though her voice said she believed us, her eyes said otherwise. "Oh, right. You've had that same costume for years."

It was true; I had worn the same cape and witch's hat at least all of high school, if not part of middle school as well. But the way she said *costume* sounded odd.

Ezra ran the bag to the kitchen, hurrying back to return to me on the couch as his mom left to go upstairs.

"Your mom knows," I whispered to him once he was next to me and his mom was out of earshot. "More than she's telling."

"You got that vibe too?"

I nodded. "That was seriously weird. Weirder than normal for her." Ezra's mom was always a little out there, but having been around her for years, it wasn't something I cared about much anymore.

"Yeah. I know. That's also why I haven't asked her about the circles yet. Something's been off about her for the past few days, since like Halloween. I thought she was sick, but Mom doesn't get sick."

Before I could answer, my phone lit up with a text.

> Miranda: Hey, there's this really cute new kid, and he's asking for your number.

> Me: New kid? When did we get a new kid?

> Miranda: Tall, handsome, perfectly sculpted cheekbones, dark hair with a white streak on the side? Have you seriously not seen him yet?

Dark hair with a white stripe? Sort of like—

"Ow!" I exclaimed, my headache returning with a vengeance. "More salve, please." Maybe going back under the pillow was a good idea, too.

I tossed the phone at Ezra and said, "Tell Miranda anyone who wants to talk to me can do so in person. Don't let her give my number out."

His fingers flew over the keyboard as I laid back down, tucking my face into the couch cushions and smothering myself with another pillow.

"Stay away from him, Cecilia. I don't think he's a good guy. He gives me the weirdest vibes."

A fresh wave of pain hit behind my eyes. I squeezed them shut and laid still, trying not to think about anything except the ocean. The imagery of gentle lapping of waves usually helped lull my brain.

After a few minutes, it subsided again. Ezra's mom called him into the kitchen to help with something, and I decided it was probably for the best that I headed home finally, where I could rest in bed the remainder of the night.

I got up, slung my backpack over my shoulder, and started for the back door to cut across the backyards. But I froze when I heard Mrs. Fallere's voice waft from the kitchen.

"I don't want you to see her anymore, Ezra. That girl is up to no good. Having you ditch school, miss your classes, always taking up your time. Your grades are slipping. You need to focus."

"Mom, I—"

"That's final, Ezra. Stay away from Cecilia Chevalier."

My heart dropped into my stomach. Mrs. Fallere thought *I* was a bad influence? I tried to be a good person. I didn't purposefully get people into trouble with me. Everything Ezra did was of his own accord. I never forced him to do anything.

But then I thought back to just the last few days. Ditching class today. The vanishing table. Rushing out of the café. The lights at school.

She was right. Maybe I was a bad influence on Ezra.

My hands began to tingle, and I knew that was my cue to leave. I turned and rushed through the front door, letting it slam behind me. I heard Ezra call my name, but didn't look back as I raced down the sidewalk.

Sidewalk.

Shoes.

Jeans.

The tingles in my fingers felt like they were going to explode, as well as my head, just as I made it to the front door.

It opened before I could reach for the handle, Gramps standing in the doorway. He took one look at me, scanning me from head to toe and back again before moving to the side and ushering me in.

"Cecilia. We need to talk."

A Snap of Secrets

CHAPTER 1

"This sucks." I snatched a French fry from Ezra's plate and shoved it into my mouth before he could grab it back. I was forever eating his fries, which was fine because I always let him have my apples.

It wasn't called a balanced diet for nothing. Just maybe not balanced for one person...

Ezra hung his head, his glasses slipping down his long nose for a second before he looked up at me over the tops of the frames and under his unruly brown hair. He really needed a haircut, but would probably wait another few weeks until he literally couldn't see anymore. It was what he did every time, and it drove me nuts.

But I wasn't one to talk. With my long, mahogany hair that reached halfway down my back, the only time I got a haircut was when it got too heavy to be in a ponytail. The headaches around the crown of my head were the first sign. It happened about every five months or so.

"I know. I'm not sure what got into my mom the other day, but she's being so unreasonable. I have an A in every class except trig, where I have a B minus. It's a B. Not even close to failing."

I tucked my lips in and stayed quiet. I had done a lot of thinking about what happened at Ezra's house over the last few days, and came to a conclusion I hadn't told him yet.

That was, I did lots of thinking *after* I slept for thirteen hours straight.

After Gramps let me into the house, he saw the pain I was in and allowed me to go to my room without the talk he wanted to give me. The next morning, he was gone, with a note on the table saying he'd be staying with his sister for a few days and to call Ezra's mom if I needed anything.

Since that day, though, the only time I saw Ezra was at school, specifically lunch. His mom locked him down, no socials, no phone outside of school, and she drove him to and from each day. We hadn't seen each other over the weekend at all, or any time outside of right now, in the past few days.

"I'm sure she'll break soon," I said, but there was no confidence behind my voice.

"Girl, you have a visitor!" Miranda announced a second later. "You said he'd have to talk to you in person…"

I froze, every cell in my body going cold at her words. "The new kid?"

Just thinking about him freaked me out. After my long, long nap, thinking about him or hearing about him didn't make my head feel like exploding anymore, but I still got a weird shiver down my spine every time.

And I still hadn't found out what happened with the three missing hours. I had been more focused on Ezra's mom and what I thought about all of that instead.

"We have bigger problems than—"

"Yeah, because look who *else* is coming this way," Miranda said in a loud whisper, interrupting Ezra, before nodding behind me.

I turned, watching Chelsea strut across the cafeteria after Xavier, a determined look on her face. She was the twin sister of the star quarterback's girlfriend, and had been single for months now. Which apparently was a sin in the cheerleader world.

I had been single for years, yet I was still doing fine. Or so I thought.

"Cecilia, please, don't. He gives me bad vibes." Ezra reached across the table and grabbed my hand, trying to get my attention away from Xavier.

The only things I had learned in the past few days were that his name was Xavier Custos, and he had just moved here from England. What part, I didn't know. Not that I would know anything about it anyway, but that was beside the point.

He was mysterious. No one knew much else about him yet. No one had even claimed to have spoken to him, except for Miranda when he asked for my number. She said after I said no, he turned and left without another word.

And now, he was now here, in front of my face, staring down at me. His dark eyes flitted between me and Ezra, settling on our joined hands for the briefest of moments before looking straight at me.

As soon as his onyx eyes connected with mine, I gasped, weird flashes appearing in my mind. It was the same things that happened when Ezra and I were hurrying to his house after leaving the nurse's office.

The darkness... like a shadow floating over my entire vision, cloaking my mind. The flat sided objects. The cold. Silhouettes of what could be people hung on the outskirts of my visualization, but it couldn't be. They were floating, moving around as if hovering inches off the ground.

Then my mind flashed again, this time to something more recognizable.

Sidewalk. Shoes. Jeans.

None of it made any sense, either apart or together. I needed more, but as soon as I tried to think about it, my head pounded, and I drew myself out of the thought. Or was it a memory?

"Cecilia?"

Dang, that English accent was going to win me over, wasn't it? Even with all my nerves firing at once, the big neon flashing sign over his head saying 'stay away,' and the fact that Ezra still hadn't let go of my hand, the way he said my name brought a sense of calm over me. It made the pounding in my head subside considerably.

"Yeah?"

Chelsea was only a few feet away now, her bright green eyes narrowed and zoned in on me.

"I was hoping maybe you and I could meet after school. At that café down the street?"

Did he say... was he asking me out? Right here in front of my friends, in front of Chelsea, who had skidded to a halt behind Xavier, her jaw dropped.

"Um, what?" His eyes found mine again and all the air left my lungs. I didn't know why I had such a visceral reaction to him every time.

Ezra's hand slipped out of mine slowly, but I didn't look over at him. Not when Xavier had me in a chokehold. Staring into his eyes was like being put through a portal—mesmerizing and entrancing.

"That café? Tea? Or coffee," he said, breaking out a half smile. It looked slightly forced, somewhere between a smile and a grimace.

That smile, though. The brilliantly white teeth. I blinked, recognizing that grin. But from where?

"She'll meet you there," Ezra interrupted, breaking whatever spell had been cast over Xavier and I.

But Xavier didn't bother looking at my best friend. He kept his gaze on me, his face turning serious once more. "If that is what Cecilia wants."

That shiver appeared again, but this time, it wasn't so foreign. It wasn't so... alarming. The warning bells weren't going off anymore. I almost felt at peace now.

"Ahem." Someone cleared their throat behind Xavier and suddenly, all the lights came back on, brighter than before, the sounds of the cafeteria ringing in my ears, deafening all other noise. "Care to explain what's going on here?"

"Well," Miranda said, pointing her French fry at Xavier, then at me, "it looks like hot new boy Xavier here just asked the lovely Cecilia Chevalier out on a date. That okay with you, Chels?"

Chels. Chelsea, the cheerleader. Right. She had been headed over here looking like a bloodhound on the trail. A trail that ended with Xavier, apparently.

Xavier finally broke, turning to glance over his shoulder. But he didn't speak. He barely gave her a half second look before turning back to me. "After school, then?"

I nodded, and as soon as he left, everything inside of me exploded. My head pounded, my heart began to race, my hands tingled more than they ever had before.

My hands tingled.

It had been days since that had happened. Not since the water fountain. Not since... not since I missed three hours of my life with no explanation.

"We need to talk. Now," I said to Ezra, as I jumped to my feet.

I didn't care that Chelsea stood there, still looking like she was in shock. I didn't care that Miranda called after me, wondering where Ezra and I were going. I didn't care that people all around stared as the two of us took off like bullets through the cafeteria.

But I did take notice that Xavier hung around the last table, right before the doors, his narrowed, hooded eyes trained on me once again.

Chapter 2

"What's wrong?" Ezra said as soon as we were sitting on the bench in the courtyard. The air had turned cold the last few days, but I needed it right now. It felt like my entire body was on fire, and the tingling traveling from my hands up my arms.

"There's something about Xavier that I can't place..." I wasn't sure where to start or what to say. This feeling was so foreign to me, I didn't know how to explain it.

"Like I said, he's bad news, CC. You need to stay away from him."

"Why?" Suddenly, a few things clicked into place. Ezra had said to stay away from him the other day at his house too, when I had him answer Miranda's text. I hadn't thought too much about it then, because of the massive migraine wrecking my body. But now, I was curious. What *did* he know about Xavier? Because besides him wanting my number, and now asking me out, I still didn't know a thing.

Except that he gave me an odd feeling when he came close. And that when his eyes locked with mine, it threw me back into that darkness, that place where I couldn't quite reach in my brain.

Maybe that was where I needed to start with Ezra. Tell him about that. The sidewalk. The shoes. The jeans. The darkness with the strange *things* coming out of the ground that I couldn't put my finger on.

Not right now, though. Now I wanted to know what Ezra had against this kid.

"Why what?"

"Why do I need to stay away from him? How do you know he's bad news?"

He shrugged and pushed his glasses up his nose. "I just do. I've heard some things. Besides, did you see him? All black clothes? The way he slinks around without making a sound? And what's up with the white hair? There's something off about him. I just don't know what. And... Well, other reasons." His cheeks flushed as he stared down at the ground.

I needed to push further. It wasn't like Ezra to judge people, especially not by their clothes and hair. "What have you heard?"

His head cocked, but he didn't meet my eyes. "Just stuff, I guess. Rumors swirl every time there's a new kid, you know?"

I didn't know. I wasn't one for gossip, and we hadn't had a new kid in the middle of the year like this in a while.

"CC, it's not that big of a deal. Go on the date. Call me if you need—" he cut himself off, remembering that he no longer could talk to me after school hours. "Call Miranda if you need backup. Actually, I'll just put her on backup to begin with. She can hang out at the café waiting for a signal or—"

"Seriously, Ez? What do you think Xavier will do, kidnap me?" Another shiver ran through me.

But Ezra didn't say anything. He didn't debate my comment. He didn't laugh at it. That worried me. Whatever it was that he knew, he wasn't telling me. He was throwing me to the wolves to let me find out on my own.

"I'll be fine. It's just coffee," I said just as the bell rang. We started for the doors, but Ezra stopped me just as we reached them.

"Last time we went for 'just coffee,' you made an entire table disappear, remember?" He didn't have to say anything else; I heard his warning loud and clear.

Which reminded me what I wanted to talk to him about, why I had dragged him from the cafeteria.

The tingling in my hands.

I hadn't used magic in a few days, a little worried that things would go awry and I would lose track of time again. Were the two things related? I didn't really think so, but also didn't want to chance it.

But ever since the tingle returned after talking to Xavier, it hadn't gone away. It was getting stronger, traveling up to my shoulders now. I couldn't ignore it any longer.

"I'll see you later?" I said as we reached the hallway.

Ezra turned and gave me the look that said, 'You know we won't.' It broke my heart, but there wasn't much I could do about it.

"See you at lunch tomorrow. I want a full report about your... *coffee date*." Then, he stepped into the crowd of students and disappeared.

I was on my own, my arms tingling, a million thoughts swirling through my mind and no direction to take them.

All I knew was I had to get rid of this feeling fast. Ducking into an empty classroom, I shut the door behind me and locked it.

I needed to focus. I couldn't go all willy-nilly on snaps, tossing them out like candy at a parade. That was how disaster struck, and I didn't need another water fountain accident. People could have been hurt with that, and it was the furthest from my intentions with my magic.

Squeezing my eyes shut, I tried to think of something small. Something that wouldn't do any damage, wouldn't hurt anyone, and would barely be noticed by anyone except me.

Think, think, think. Focus, CC, focus.

Then, I got it. Something small in the classroom. The plain, boring, dull classroom. It needed some livening up. And what better way to liven the room up than with a vase of fresh flowers?

Whoever the teacher was that used this room next would surely appreciate them.

I waited until I could clearly see a vase with flowers sitting on the desk in front of me in my mind. By then, the tingle had spread to my chest, still working its way down through my body.

"Here goes nothing," I whispered to myself.

Snap snap.

I peeked one eye open, excited to see a glass vase with a dozen red roses on the teacher's desk. What I wasn't excited about was the tingle that remained coursing through my body. It was like being tickled from the inside out.

I sighed. So much for that idea. It had worked last time, even if the magic had backfired.

Then I figured one more vase couldn't hurt. One more attempt to see if I could get this feeling to go away. There was no way I could focus on the rest of my school day if I didn't.

Once again, I closed my eyes, even though I wasn't sure if that was necessary, and thought about the flowers.

Snap snap.

I waited a moment before looking, taking an extra breath and hoping.

Oh no. Ohhhhhh no.

I smelled it before I saw it. The overwhelming scent of roses filled my nose just as my eyes flew open to witness the chaos.

Roses. Vases and vases of roses *everywhere*. They covered every flat surface in the room, dozens upon dozens of flowers.

I glanced around wildly, trying to figure out what to do about this. It wasn't a horrible problem to have. Too many flowers never hurt anyone. They made people happy.

But whoever used this classroom next probably wouldn't be happy to find absolutely no space for themselves or the students.

As a last-ditch effort, I found a paper and a pen and scribbled a note, leaving it balancing precariously on top of one of the roses on the teacher's desk.

Have a fantastic day! Love, your secret admirer.

It was corny. Cheesy. Gimmicky. Potentially a little stalkerish, but at this particular moment, I didn't care. I just needed to leave before anyone saw me.

Whirling around, I headed toward the door, but not before I saw a streak of black dash in front of the window next to the door.

My face paled. Someone had been watching. I flew to the door, opening it and sticking my head out, looking from side to side to see who it had been.

But all I saw was a pair of jeans and black sneakers rounding the corner and out of sight.

Sidewalk. Shoes. Jeans.

It all flashed through my mind again, because of what I had just seen.

Those shoes were the same shoes from whatever the darkness was in my mind. Whether a memory or a figment of my imagination, I wasn't sure.

But now I knew who they belonged to. Without a doubt.

CHAPTER 3

"I know you saw me," was the first thing out of my mouth after I sat down at the table in front of Xavier.

I had left him waiting for almost ten extra minutes as I paced outside the café. The decision to come had been easy, especially after I realized he was the person watching me through the classroom window. But actually sitting down with him, having a conversation?

It scared the pants off of me. I still couldn't figure out what it was about him that both thrilled and terrified me in equal proportions.

Could I do a quick snappity snap and get rid of him? Potentially. But I wouldn't. There had to be some reason Ezra wanted me to stay far away. Some reason Xavier was following me.

And now, I also knew there was some reason he was connected to the darkness in my mind. The flashes I only seemed to see when I thought about or was around him lately.

Sidewalk. Shoes. Jeans.

His shoes. His jeans? And what sidewalk?

We stared at each other, him not blinking, not wavering in the slightest. Nothing in his facial expression gave him away. He was as still as a statue, unmoving and silent.

"You saw me. You were watching me. You've *been* watching me," I clarified at the end. Just as I did, pain erupted in my head again. The darkness showed up, but this time, it wasn't the same place. In the distance, I could barely make out a hallway at school. It was like I had tunnel vision, unable to see the big picture, just a brief moment in time, far, far away.

My hand flew to my forehead, clutching it, trying to relieve the pain as I grimaced and squeezed my eyes shut. A second later, my other hand, lying flat on the table, pushing down as if to relieve the pain by another pressure point, became ice cold as something rested on top of it.

I flinched, but the coldness didn't go away. Instead, the tunnel in my mind grew bigger and bigger. The pain lessened, and that's when I saw—

Xavier.

Over Miranda's shoulder.

The day the water fountain exploded.

Xavier had been there, down the hall. As soon as I had seen him, he left. But then... after the water incident, he was there again. And I... I... I...

The darkness disappeared, as did all the pain.

"I'm sorry," Xavier said.

My eyes flew open. "Say that again."

"I'm sorry." He didn't elaborate. He didn't say *what* he was sorry for. But I *knew* that from somewhere. I had heard him say it before.

I lowered my hand off of my head and to the table. That's when I saw it—his hand, laying over mine, the coldness coming from him.

"Your hand... it's freezing." *Why* was his hand so cold? And why did it help my memory to open up, to make the pain go away?

"In due time, everything will become clear," he whispered, snatching his hand away and circling it around his cup.

His cup. He had a cup of coffee. Maybe tea. But there was another one close to him. A plastic cup, with a blended beverage in it.

"For you," he said after catching me looking at it. "Your friend Miranda said it was your usual." He lifted his chin and nodded across the café. I whirled around and looked, finding her sitting in the armchairs in the far corner.

"Ezra," I muttered to myself, knowing full well he told her to come spy on me.

"She is quite the character, that one. Wanted to know my full life history down to my blood type before allowing me inside these doors." Xavier lifted his cup to his lips, a sly smile crossing them.

"She gets like that sometimes," I answered while reaching across the table for my drink. "Thank you for this. But it probably was because of Ezra. My friend at lunch?"

Xavier's eyes darkened, if that was even possible due to how black they already were. "Ezra."

I nodded. I couldn't keep eye contact with him for long. "Yeah. He doesn't like you." Bluntness was a personality trait. "He said he's heard some things about you and didn't really want me to come."

Xavier nodded, as if he had heard that a million times before. "Ezra doesn't know me. Rumors are just that—rumors. Usually based in fiction, if I must say."

I stayed silent for a moment, and so did he. Xavier seemed like a guy of few words to begin with, but also one of those that didn't feel the need to silence with senseless conversation.

The complete opposite of me.

"What—why—I need to—what about—"

"One thing at a time, Cecilia," Xavier said softly. How he said my name... it was like it instantly calmed me. My body and mind had been on high alert since the moment I saw him outside the classroom, but now... it all stopped. Except for the tingles. Those had only gotten worse, now almost to my knees. Soon, my entire body would be one giant electric static.

"What did you do just now?" That was the most recent issue, so I put it first. "How did you get the pain to stop?"

I purposefully left out the part where it seemed like his touch also opened my mind, allowing me to see through that tunnel, to the part where I saw him in the hallway staring back at me.

"Only thou who hath caused thy pain can be thy cure," he said so quietly, I thought I imagined it. But there was no way I could imagine *that*.

The way it sounded in his accent, the way he hid half behind his cup, the way it sounded like English, but also... not. All of it together made no sense.

"What did you just say?"

"You heard it. You understood it."

I shook my head, leaning forward and resting my elbows on the table, my head in my hands. My auburn hair fell around me like a curtain, blocking everything out as I rubbed at my temples.

"You... *you* caused the pain and therefore only you could take it away?"

He didn't answer. I glanced up, finding him staring expectedly at me.

"You... you were there. The day of the water fountain explosion. Down the hall, I saw you. And then again, when... when..." It was *right there* at the edge of my mind, but I couldn't reach it. The more I tried to think about it, the further it slipped away into the darkness.

"Cecilia," Xavier whispered. "Don't fight it. It'll come in due time."

"What does that *mean*?" The tingle intensified as I grew more and more frustrated. Why wouldn't he just come out and tell me what was going on?

"Be curious, Cecilia. Ask questions. Don't take anything for granted."

"The classroom. You saw me in the classroom," I burst out, suddenly wanting to know the answer to everything.

Xavier nodded, wrapping his hands around his cup again, but otherwise not moving.

"You saw... the flowers." My pulse quickened. Xavier's eyes searched my face, flickering to my lips, my neck, and back to my eyes. As soon as we connected again, the pain returned.

I lowered a hand, hoping he would take it.

He did. Instantly.

As soon as his frigid fingers found mine, the pain disappeared.

"Cecilia, there are many things in this life you may not understand. And many more to come." Was I imagining things, or did he sound a little exasperated? Like he was frustrated with me for not knowing whatever it was he thought I didn't understand.

Because there was a *lot* I didn't understand about this new life of mine. A lot I wasn't sure I would ever understand.

"Is that why you asked me here? Because you know... you know *what I am*?" I lowered my voice at the end, not wanting anyone else to overhear.

Xavier's hand squeezed against mine slightly, making me realize he had yet to let go. Considering the pain that hit my head when he did, I almost didn't want him to.

"Of course I know." There he went with that tone again. It was getting old, fast.

"What *else* do you know?" I asked.

But he just shook his head and took his hand back. "That is not a conversation for here."

I leaned back in my chair, letting my hands drop into my lap, staring at him dumbfoundedly. "So let's go then."

"Not now."

"When? Why? Where? You seem to be evoking more questions than you give answers today."

The corner of his lip lifted, and he broke out into a small smile with those gleaming white teeth again. "In due time, Cecilia."

I huffed. "Would you stop saying that? You sound like an eighty-year-old man. What is due time, anyway? Who decides that?"

Xavier chuckled, a low, deep rumbling sound emitting from his chest. I found myself smiling, a happiness filling my chest, slowly radiating throughout my body.

"You are not what I expected, Cecilia Chevalier. Let's go for a walk, shall we?"

Part of me wanted to jump up and follow him wherever he went. The other part still had the neon sign saying stay away flashing in front of her face.

"Where? And is that a good thing or a bad thing? What did you expect? And why were you expecting something?" Again, more questions than answers from the guy dressed in all black in front of me.

"Anywhere." Xavier stood and pushed his chair back, then extended his hand to me. He didn't bother answering any of my other questions, which at this point didn't shock me.

Against what was probably my better judgment, I took it and stood, grabbing my drink with my other hand. Before we left, I glanced over my shoulder at Miranda. She gave me a thumbs up and waved.

Chapter 4

"So you know I'm a witch," I blurted out when we were alone. Xavier had let go of my hand after we pushed through the door, but I found myself once again wishing he hadn't.

"I do."

"Why did you run away then? Why didn't you come into the classroom or wait for me to leave?"

Xavier shoved his hands into his pockets. He had left his coffee or tea or whatever he had been drinking behind at the café like an afterthought. I clung tightly to mine, even though it was making my hands cold.

He let out a heavy sigh before answering my question. Somehow, I felt like I had become some sort of burden to him, like I was doing a disservice, even though *he* had asked *me* out. "Because you needed to reveal yourself to me first. Like you just did."

My brows furrowed. "Reveal myself? To you? Why? What does that do?"

He pointed at a bench under a large, shady tree. "It does a lot. More than you can imagine right now."

"Well, tell me one thing then." So far, he had given me nothing. Except taking the pain away. That was nice. Other than that, he had yet to explain anything, and had only been adding to my questions over the afternoon.

"Revealing yourself as a witch to me means I can give you back your memories."

I froze halfway to sitting on the bench. He had waited, allowing me to sit first, so he stood, watching me hover in mid-air. I plopped down onto the wood with a thud. "Excuse me?"

Xavier lifted his dark gray pea coat slightly away from his torso so he could sit next to me. "But not now. Not until you can understand."

"Enlighten me, then." This guy was *really* getting on my nerves. Despite his looks, his gentlemanly ways, his accent, and the way he could instantly calm me and take pain away, he bothered me.

"Cecilia, there is an entire *world* you are unaware of. I was not made aware just *how* unaware you were." He whispered the last part under his breath, but I still heard him loud and clear. So he *was* bothered by me. Apparently by my lack of understanding of everything going on with me at the moment, which also, same.

"Bombarding you with information too soon will lead to drastic consequences. I am unwilling to damage you further, so for now, why don't we speak about the sensation you are feeling through your body?"

The sensation... "The tingles?" How did he know about the tingles? "Wait, back up. Damage me *further*?"

His lips quirked at that, but once again avoided answering the more important question. "Tingles, you call it? Interesting. Accurate, but interesting. Yes. The tingles, Cecilia. Tell me about the tingles."

"You know about the tingles..." I whispered, still trying to wrap my brain around it. "Are you a witch too? Ezra said—"

"Ezra said what?" Xavier interrupted quickly, almost *too* quickly, and in almost a brutal tone. I looked up at him, his eyes practically glowing on the outer rims of the onyx irises.

"Said that only the women in the circles were witches. The guys weren't witches. Or wizards. Or whatever the term is."

Xavier's jaw tightened. "Ezra is correct. But he only knows what he can read about. Don't trust him for everything."

I scanned Xavier then, blatantly and openly. "And I should trust *you*? Why you instead of the best friend I've had forever?"

His nod was slow and long. "I can't tell you why, but yes. You should trust me."

"You stole my memories."

"I've hidden some of your memories," he clarified, as if it were any better.

My jaw literally dropped. "You... you... *what*?"

"Not now, Cecilia. There isn't much time. Tell me where the... *tingles* are?"

There wasn't *time*? I had all the time in the world! I would stay out all night if it meant figuring out what this boy wanted and how he knew all these things.

But I started by answering what he wanted. "It started in my hands," I said, holding them up and showing them to him as if he had never seen hands before.

"Mhm."

"That was it for a while."

"Until?"

"Until... the water fountain day. They started tingling really bad."

"What did you do?"

"Snapped. And the fountain exploded." I wasn't even embarrassed. He didn't sound like he was judging me. Besides, if he knew I was a witch already, he wouldn't laugh.

"And then?"

And then I lost three hours of my life, which you seem to know what happened but won't tell me, is what I wanted to say. But I kept my mouth shut on that. He wanted to know about the tingles, so the tingles I would tell him.

"And then I didn't feel it for a while. A few days, at least. Not until today. At lunch."

That slow nod returned, his eyes cutting to mine.

"When you...asked me out?" Wow, that sounded dumber than I hoped it would. With all he'd told me, and not told me, so far, it really didn't seem like this was a date anymore. It was a group meeting. Informational exchange. Anything but a date.

"Then they came back?"

"With a vengeance. I haven't been able to get rid of it."

"Has it expanded?"

"Down to my knees now."

"And conjuring vases of flowers?"

"Didn't help." I shook my head, thinking about all those flowers. I looked up at Xavier, finding a contemplative and calm look on his otherwise pale face. Was he always that pale or was it just a reflection off of his dark hair and clothes?

"Hmm," he said, as if he were expecting that.

"You haven't answered my question." My heart was still pounding, the tingles spreading further.

"Which was that?"

"Are you also a witch or whatever the male equivalent is?" This time, I held his gaze, not wanting him to find a way out of this answer. I needed some sort of stability right now, and the way he kept dodging answers while making more questions frustrated me.

Xavier barely blinked as he looked back, that same brilliant grin stretching across his face. "What do you think, Cecilia?"

I... I... I didn't know *what* to think. All I knew was that my heart wouldn't stop hammering against my ribs and my mouth went dry. Even the tingles subsided for a brief second.

"I'm not sure," I whispered back.

"What has your grandfather told you?"

If I had my cup in my hand, it would have been on the floor. "My grandfather? How do you know I live with my grandfather? What does he have to do with any of this?"

Xavier tucked his lips in and closed his eyes briefly. "Cecil-ia..."

If he got to be frustrated with me, then I was allowed to be frustrated with him. "No, don't you *Cecilia* me. Besides, I go by CC. And leave Gramps out of whatever this craziness is you're doing. Hiding memories. Somehow damaging me, which you still haven't explained. Look, I don't know who you are or where you came from or why you know so much about me, but this is creepy." I sat up, wanting to leave, but for some reason I was frozen in place.

"You were not what I expected, considering... Well, in any manner, there is much to learn. Be wise with your choices, Cecilia."

Anger grew within me. Be wise with my choices? In due time? Thou, hath, thy? Who was this guy?

We both sat there, looking at each other for another few moments, absolutely transfixed with one another. Or at least, I was transfixed with him. I physically couldn't look away. He infuriated me and captivated me at the same time.

Eventually, Xavier spoke first. "I must go. Thank you for meeting with me. It was... enlightening." Xavier stood, breaking the connection between us. The loss was felt instantly. Once again, he lowered his hand to help me to my feet.

I took it a lot faster than I had the last time, holding tight as he lifted me up. The second I was in front of him, my head practically split into two.

Darkness.

Sidewalk. Shoes. Jeans.

Gates. Big, iron gates.

Falling.

Xavier's face staring down at me.

Flying. No, gliding? No. Running.

Sidewalk. Shoes. Jeans.

Tabletops. No... *gravestones*? The tall, flat sided objects were gravestones.

Xavier's face again, looking at me with a mix of concern and contemplativeness. He was so close, mere inches away.

I was in his arms. He was carrying me around gravestones. Darkness.

Sidewalk. Shoes. Jeans.

Xavier's shoes. Xavier's jeans. The sidewalk. Gates. The cemetery.

"Cecilia. Cecilia, it's not time yet." Xavier's voice broke through the fog, the darkness. The icy cold from his fingers hit my head, jolting me back to reality.

"Cecilia."

I blinked, looking at him, still so close to me. Except this time, I wasn't in his arms. I was back on the bench, and he was sitting next to me, his hands still on my face, the pads of his long fingers pressing on my temples.

"I'm sorry, Cecilia."

Every time he said my name it felt like my heart wanted to burst out of my chest. "Sorry?"

"It's not time yet. That wasn't supposed to happen. Please accept my apologies, but I cannot answer your questions about what you just saw. Try to forget it. For now."

Forget it? He wanted me to forget what I saw? When it finally came back to me, albeit in pieces? There was no way.

"I must go. In due time, Cecilia Chevalier. In due time, it will all become clear. Until then, keep this. Try not to think about what you saw, as I will not be here to take the pain away."

He reached up and unclasped something from around his neck. A necklace. I hadn't even known he had been wearing one, stuck underneath his black shirt.

He dropped it into my hands, wrapping my fingers around it and giving it a squeeze. "It'll protect you. To an extent."

And then, he was gone. He took off down the street and hung a right at the corner, out of sight in seconds.

CHAPTER 5

I didn't open my hands until I made it home. The splitting in my head had subsided when Xavier touched my face, but didn't completely disappear. It was more like a dull throbbing.

But he was also right. Every time I tried to think about the flashes I saw, the cemetery, being in his arms, it hurt more and more.

Oddly enough, thinking about this afternoon, being with Xavier, didn't have the same effect.

As soon as I got to my room, I looked at the necklace. A silver medallion type charm hung on a long, plain silver chain with no clasp. There wasn't a lot of weight to it, the medallion rather flat. But there was a symbol engraved on it, or maybe stamped? I wasn't well versed in jewelry making. Nor could I tell what the symbol was. It looked like squiggles of lines intersecting, like letters or maybe even a snake. There was no color on it, it was all silver with the squiggles raised, almost looking embossed.

The squiggles looked like the small scar I had on my wrist. They, too, were squiggle-ish, but not the same as the ones on the necklace.

But that was it. Just a charm on a chain, nothing more.

Unsure what it meant, I slid it around my neck, tugging on it slightly to make sure it was secure.

Instantly, the tingles disappeared. Vanished. They had almost hit my ankles a moment ago, and now it was gone.

But my body wasn't completely void of feeling, though. It was more like... an electric buzz humming low, deep beneath the surface. I knew it was there, but it wasn't as overwhelming as the tingle.

"Cecilia!" Gramps' voice echoed through the house. I hadn't expected him to be home, even though his note said he would only be gone for a few days.

"Upstairs! Be down in a second!"

I ran a brush through my hair and washed my hands, both out of habit. Gramps always made me do both things whenever I got home from school, ever since I was a little girl.

He stood by the front door, shuffling through the stack of mail from the past few days. He must have collected what was in the box today too, as I hadn't thought to grab it when I came in.

"Hi! Did you have a good trip? To... er, where exactly did you go?" I knew what he wrote on the note, but if he slipped up, it would tell me he was lying. Not that I was looking to catch him in a lie, but the way he said we needed to talk, and then up and disappeared? Suspicious.

"To visit my sister, like I said." He huffed at all the junk mail in his hands before looking up. His eye instantly caught the necklace on my chest. I reached up to grab it, to put it under my shirt, but he stopped me, blocking my arm. "Where did you get that?" he snapped.

I froze. "Um, a friend?"

"How long have you had it?"

"Literally just got it like ten minutes ago, Gramps. Why?"

"Who gave it to you?"

I took a step back and frowned. "I said to a friend."

"Ezra?"

"No. A new friend, Xavier Custos."

The second his name left my lips, Gramps hand fell to his side, and he swayed slightly. I reached out and steadied him, grasping him by the arm and helping him to the couch.

"Gramps, are you okay? What's going on?" I sat down next to him and grabbed the bottle of water I had left on the side table last night, uncapping it before handing it over.

But he swatted me away and pushed to sit. His face seemed paler than normal, his wrinkles more pronounced. But his sparkling blue eyes lifted to meet mine.

"Cecilia. There are things you don't know about our family. About your mother and your gramma," he started, his voice a little horse or even choked up. He often struggled when talking about his wife.

"Actually... I know." I held up my hand and looked at the fireplace. Conjuring flames? No, bad idea. I could burn the entire house down. Turning, I glanced at the TV. That could be easy enough.

I focused hard, but the tingles never came. Not wanting to waste any time, I stared at the TV and snapped twice.

The evening news burst onto the screen, the volume up as loud as Gramps usually listened to it.

Yet, there was still no tingle. The low-lying hum electrified through my bones, but the tingle was gone. How did that just work without the tingle?

My hand flew to the necklace under my shirt. Ever since I put it on, the overwhelming feeling had subsided, but I didn't think it would also disappear while I snapped.

"And so you do. So you do. I suspected it, which was why I went to my sister's..."

The inner light bulb finally clicked on. Gramp's *sister*. If Gramma was a witch, maybe Great Aunt Pearl was too. I mean, it seemed a bit unlikely, since the circle was from Gramma's family, but it could be...

"No, Cecilia, she isn't a witch. But she knew about your Gramma, your mom, the whole line. It was hard to hide, but there are certain people that are allowed to know. Within reason," he said, as if he could read my mind.

I collapsed onto the couch next to him, staring up at him like I had when I was little. It had been just him and I for all of my life. We sat here almost every night, with him telling me stories about his life when he was young, when he was with Gramma, or very occasionally, about Mom. Or we just sat here while he watched the news. I would read or watch with him.

"There's a lot I don't know. But Ezra's been doing some research, because it seems like he has an ancestor—"

"Ezra? Doing research into the family circle?" Gramps bushy gray brows raised in surprise.

"Yeah..." I dragged out, pausing to see if he wanted to say anymore.

He didn't.

"Technically, he was looking into his family first, and found rumors one of his ancestors was a witch. Then... well, then Halloween happened, and I showed him what I could do and—"

"He knows? Ezra knows?"

I frowned. "Of course he knows. He's my best friend. Who else would I have told?"

Xavier, that's who. But he seemed to know even before I said anything. Whether he knew before he saw me in the classroom or after, I wasn't sure.

"Cecilia, listen to me. It is imperative that you do not tell Ezra more than he already knows." The firmness in Gramps' voice made me sit up straight.

"Why?"

Gramp's blue eyes stared at me with an intensity I had never seen before. He paused, like he was trying to figure something out. "Just do as I say, okay?"

I let out a breath and looked down. "I mean, yeah. But..."

"But what?"

"Well, the other day, you know when I came home with the migraine, um, his mom sort of forbade him to hang out with me anymore."

Gramps leapt to his feet. "Why?"

"I don't know!" I shrugged. "I think she knows something about their family circle and just wants Ezra to stay away? She said it was because I was a bad influence on him because we, um, well, kind of skipped school."

But it didn't seem like Gramps was concerned about the skipping. He already knew I missed part of the day, anyway. "I think it's for the best as well. Just for now."

With that, he turned and walked out of the living room and into his bedroom, shutting the door behind him.

The TV still blared in the corner. I looked at it and snapped twice. It shut off instantly.

"At least I have that going for me," I muttered. I reached up and took the necklace out from under my shirt. "If no one is willing to tell me anything, then I'll have to do it all myself, won't I?"

CHAPTER 6

I made sure to tuck Xavier's necklace under my shirt again before leaving for school the next morning. Not only did I not want Gramps asking about it, but I wasn't in the mood to tell anyone else either.

Ezra never caught up with me like he normally did. His mom probably drove him, which was fine. He would only want to ask about my date with Xavier, and there was nothing I could tell him.

According to Gramps, there was nothing I should be telling him anyway. For some reason, both Ezra's mom and Gramps wanted us to stay away from each other, for reasons unknown.

Well, really, Gramps just didn't want me talking to Ezra about my witchiness. He didn't say I had to stay away from him. So that was the plan.

But before I could put that plan into action, I had to get through Miranda.

"Oh. My. Gosh. How was it? When you guys left, I was all like 'go get 'em tiger,' but then I was like, oh man, maybe I should have followed? Ezra wanted to make sure you were okay, because he has some weird vibe about Xavier, and I get it, he's looking out for you. But man oh man, the way Xavier looked at you at the café? I need to find me one of those."

I tilted my head, waiting to see when she was going to take a breath. Obviously, I couldn't tell her anything real about the date either, so I just stood there until she finished.

"So, spill! What happened when you guys left?"

I shrugged. "Nothing. He walked me home."

Lies, lies, lies. One day they would catch up to me.

"Okay, but it was like the perfect first date, right? I mean, I interfered slightly, telling him your favorite drink, but he was waiting for you. With your favorite drink. And the two of you totally hit it off! I could tell, even from across the café." Miranda desperately wanted me to tell her something that confirmed her suspicions, so I did the best I could.

"Yeah. That accent? The whole bad boy vibe going on? I mean... chills." At least that part was true. When I saw Xavier, I definitely got chills. Shivers. Not tingles, but close enough. She just didn't need to know *why* I got a shiver.

Mainly because I still didn't know myself. And I was getting a little tired of *not* knowing things.

If I couldn't talk to Ezra about it, and I didn't want to be seen talking to Xavier in front of people, then it would be up to me to figure things out on my own. I had no idea where to even start, but it needed to be done.

"Oh, there he is! Are you guys going on another date?" Miranda clutched my arm, bouncing on her toes.

"I don't think so," I whispered, dragging the words out as I searched the hall for him. It didn't take long before his dark eyes found mind.

Except this time, when we connected, my head didn't burst out into a massive amount of pain. Even from across the hall I saw his quick glance down at my neck. I raised my hand and touched the necklace under my shirt.

He knew. He knew I was wearing it. I didn't know why he had given it to me, but he said it would protect me. From what was still a mystery.

"Come on, Cecilia! You have to go on another date! You two would be so cute together."

"Why do you say that?"

She stopped and lifted a finger to her lips. "Honestly, I don't know. A gut feeling? A vibe?"

"What do you know about him?"

"Nothing. No one knows anything about him," Ezra cut in, scaring both of us. I jumped and turned toward him, taking a small step away at first.

Something was off. There was some weird tension between us, one I could sense right away. It made me nervous, scared almost.

"Ezra! Don't go around scaring me like that." I tried to play it off, but he wasn't buying it.

"I watched her for you, Ez. She had a great time. Xavier was nothing but a gentleman," Miranda said before heading off toward her locker before class.

"Great. Literally not what I wanted to hear, but whatever. I need to talk to you." Ezra's face was tense as he reached to grab my arm, trying to pull me toward him and out of the middle of the hall.

But the second he laid a hand on my arm, it felt like my entire arm was on *fire*. Like his hand scalded me even from over my sweater.

"Ah!" I cried, pulling away. Ezra let go, frowning, his brows furrowing behind his glasses.

"What just happened?"

"I'm not sure."

He shook his head and reached for me again, but he didn't even get close before I jumped away. This time, he didn't need to touch me for it to hurt; the moment he got within a few inches, heat started rising.

But it wasn't only on my arm. The necklace under my shirt began to warm up at the same time, pressing into my chest with its heat.

"Cecilia... what is going on?"

"Ezra, I just said I *don't know*."

His eyes narrowed, like he didn't believe I was telling the truth. Which was annoying, because I was. I didn't know why his touch suddenly felt like burning.

"This has Xavier's name written all over it. What did you tell him? What did he say to you yesterday?"

Now I really took a step back. "Are you kidding? Are you... Ezra, are you *jealous* or something?"

He whipped his head toward me so fast, I thought he broke his neck. The snarl on his lips was both devastating and terrifying. "Me? Jealous? Of him? Absolutely not."

The bell rang, interrupting what I wanted to ask next, so I let it go for now. "See you at lunch?"

"Yeah. And Cecilia?" Ezra went to reach out again, but stopped before he got close, his arm hanging in the air between us. "We really need to talk. Don't go snapping before then, okay?"

Chapter 7

I tried to follow his directions. I really, truly did.

But when Chemistry came around again, and we were back in the lab, I was bound and determined not to leave with green goo all over me again. I wanted to prove myself, wanted to show that I could do something right for a change.

Besides, what kind of witch was I if I couldn't brew a potion? Wasn't that all Chemistry really was, brewing potions? We followed a recipe of sorts, added ingredients, and stirred, waiting for the final results.

The ingredients might not have been wart of a newt or hair of a child, but it had to be simple enough.

"And how are we today?" Matt asked, leaning his elbows on the lab table and waggling his eyebrows at me.

Of course Miranda probably told him about the date with Xavier yesterday. Those two were such gossips.

"*We*," I said, making sure to emphasize the word and gesture between the two of us, "are doing great. *We* are going to get this potion, er, experiment done right today."

His brows lifted. "Oh are we now? I mean, yeah, that's the goal, but not usually the end result for the pair of us. What's changed?"

I looked at him as I slipped on my safety goggles and rolled up my sleeves. "Sheer determination not to flunk a course I should be acing."

"You? Acing? When was the last time you aced a class, CC? Fourth grade?"

I pursed my lips and pretended to read the instruction sheet in front of me. He wasn't wrong. I wasn't a straight A kind of kid; that was Ezra. He was great at making sure I didn't fail any classes, but had given up on getting me to get anything higher than a B in middle school.

Which was probably another reason his mom wanted me to stay away. Any more togetherness, and she probably thought I would bring down his entire grade point average.

"Well, nothing like the present to make some changes." Now was my chance. I had to focus, get the tingle, and snap before we started working. This would take some intense concentration, because it would be the first time I tried to change something *before* it happened.

I wanted Matt and I to understand the instructions and do the experiment correctly. I didn't want us to fail and then have me snappity snap for the correct result. All I needed was to give us a little boost, a little more effort in the right direction.

The more I stared at the sheet on the table, the hazier my vision went, like I was dissociating or something. The necklace on my chest warmed slightly, but not to a point where it hurt. More like it was feeding off the energy inside of me, the constant hum that was always in the background.

Glancing between the sheet, the vials, the ingredients, and Matt, I lifted my hands, ready. "You know what," I said to Matt, trying to work the snaps in seamlessly, "why don't you read the sheet and I'll... I'll... Oh, I'll grab the beakers from Mrs. Chung's table!"

Snap snap.

I cued them so it worked with me getting a thought. I froze at first, hesitating, my whole body waiting for something bad to happen.

"CC? Are you still with me here? You know I can't do this one alone." Matt snapped in front of my face and I about had a heart attack.

"Don't!" I grabbed his hands and pulled them down, almost pulling his whole body across the table. "I mean, sorry. But you know the rules—no reaching across the table!"

He withdrew his hands quickly, looking a bit sheepish. "Gotcha. Anyway, step one..."

Twenty minutes later, we were done. The first group done at that. Plus, nothing exploded, spilled, overflowed, blew up, or otherwise went wrong.

We both stared at the beaker, the liquid the correct color, not smoking, on fire, or in a solid state.

"We... did it?" Matt said slowly, as if he didn't want to jinx it.

I nodded, unable to speak.

"Mrs. Chung! We finished!" he called, waving the teacher over to us.

She glanced over her shoulder, then did a double take when she saw it was us. Her gaze flicked down to the beaker, and she paused, her eyes widening.

A slow smile spread across my face. We did it. Matt and I successfully completed a Chemistry experiment without failing.

Mrs. Chung took her time examining our work, looking over everything and asking a ton of questions. We weren't offended in the slightest, however.

"Well done, you two. I think this is your first A+ work. Clean it up and I'll see you next class. I don't know what changed, but I'm proud of you both."

Matt and I beamed at each other. Once we left the class, early for the first time ever, Matt looked at me and asked, "Okay, what sort of witchcraft did you do to get us to accomplish *that*?"

I froze on the spot. "What? I mean... Wha—what?"

"Man, my mom is going to be happy. Having a son who gets a C in Chemistry when you're a college science professor is really a let-down for her sometimes. But now I can go home and boast for a week straight! All thanks to you!"

"But... there was no witchcraft. Just us focusing and... um... and... yeah, just put in the work today, I guess."

Matt stared at me for a moment before putting the back of his hand against my forehead. "You okay? You seem a little pale and kinda sweaty." He wiped his hand off on his jeans.

"No, I'm fine. Just... yeah, I'm okay. Shocked we did that." I jerked my thumb over my shoulder toward class. "I hope your mom goes all out and bakes you a cake and everything!"

He laughed. "She better. Baking is the same as Chemistry, basically. Except now that we got that A, she's going to keep wanting A's. She might even ask me to help do the baking..."

"Don't bring me the leftovers," I chided, bumping my shoulder into his.

He agreed and turned to go down another hallway toward his next class while I continued on straight.

That had gone well. *Really* well. Probably one of my best snaps to date. What if Xavier's necklace amplified my powers somehow? What if it made it so all my snaps worked exactly how I wanted them to?

There was only one way to test that theory.

My mind flashed back to Ezra, to him telling me not to do any magic until he could talk to me. I obviously didn't listen, and nothing bad had happened.

So... what if I just experimented a little more? Maybe I was on a good luck streak for once. Instead of being the girl that crazy things always happen to, I could become the girl who always had great luck. Except it wouldn't be luck, it would be—

Ooof.

"Eeps!"

A hand caught me before I made it to the floor. As soon as it did, my head burst into pain and I clutched it while being raised to my feet.

"Ow! What—"

Faster than I could blink, fingers were on my temple. Ridiculously *cold* fingers. Half a second later, the pain was gone.

Why had there been pain in the first place? I hadn't even fallen, much less hit my head. And I hadn't thought of—

Xavier.

CHAPTER 8

The icy cold fingers belonged to Xavier. He pulled me off to the side of the hallway against the lockers and stared down at me with his dark, black eyes.

"You need to watch where you're going. This isn't the first time you've run into me."

"It's not the…" I trailed off, my mind catching up. A memory flashed through my brain, of me on my butt, looking up at Xavier from his shoes to his jeans to—

Sidewalk. Shoes. Jeans.

"Okay, this has *got* to stop. I'm going to need some actual answers here. Between you, my gramps, Ezra, all I've been given are vague thoughts and opinions and a whole bunch of *nothing*."

Xavier didn't say a word. He just continued to stare at me, but I wasn't going to let that slide.

"What memory are you giving back now? What pain did you inflict that you're taking back?"

"I already said—this isn't the first time you bumped into me. Now a question for you—what did your grandfather say to you?"

My cheeks flushed, and I looked down at the floor. "Not much. Just… that I shouldn't be talking to Ezra about wi—about you know what. Which seemed odd because Ezra's mom had already told him he had to stay away from me. But neither adult will say *why*. And then this morning, Ezra said

I shouldn't go around snapping today until he could tell me something important. But he didn't have a chance."

Xavier's jaw tightened when I mentioned Ezra, but he stayed quiet.

"It's fine, though, because I only did it once, and it was for the greater good. My friend Matt and I really needed some extra focus in Chemistry today, and that was what I went for. Focus. I didn't snap for a different grade or for the experiment to be done for us—"

"You used your... you know... in front of mortals?"

"Mortals? Really?"

A low growl escaped from Xavier's throat, but he didn't expand on the thought.

"Well... sort of. I mean I have been? Experimenting, really. Just small things. *Most* of them end up fine, but there was the thing with the lights, and the water fountain and—"

Pain hit my skull again when I mentioned the water fountain. In an instant, Xavier's hands were on my face once more.

"This needs to stop. Whatever it is, I need it to stop."

"In due time, Cecilia."

The way he said my name... there was something about it. The way it instantly calmed me down, the way it made me feel safe and loved. All with one word.

"There was one thing, though..." As Xavier dropped his hands, the pain disappeared, but it reminded me of what happened with Ezra this morning. "This? It gets, um, hot."

I pointed to my chest, then took the necklace out to show him I was wearing it.

His eyes went wide. "When *exactly* did it get hot?"

My heart began to pound as I slipped it back under my shirt. Xavier grabbed my other wrist, holding it tightly in his hand. "This morning, when I was talking to Ezra. He went to reach for my arm, like you're doing now, and it... it felt like someone burned me. Even through my shirt. And then when he tried again, my arm felt hot before he even touched me. Then the necklace got warm, and it was all just so weird."

Xavier's grip tightened, and he pulled me closer to him. We were inches away from each other now. "This happened when you were talking to Ezra? The one whose mother refuses to let him see you?"

I frowned, my brows furrowed in concentration and confusion. "Yes?"

Xavier remained silent.

"Is this bad? This is bad. I know it's bad. You wouldn't be making that growly scrowly face if this wasn't bad. How bad is it? Am I... am I going to *die*?" I whispered at the end, staring up at his dark eyes with my wide ones.

After he processed what I had said, one side of his mouth curved up into what I could almost consider a smile. "Growly scrowly?"

That's what he took from my comments? "Yeah. How else do you describe your permanent frown and the wrinkles you'll undoubtedly have between your brows in twenty years?"

"I won't."

"Sure you will. But not the point. How bad is this?" I pointed to the necklace, now not hot at all. But the rest of me was. I was flushed from head to toe, both with a bit of embarrassment and... well I wasn't sure what the other part was.

"You're not going to die. Not on my watch," Xavier said.

"On your watch? What are you, my bodyguard? My stalker?" The bell rang, reminding me that Matt and I had gotten out of class early. Everyone else was coming out now, which meant... "Wait, why weren't you in class just now?"

"Because I'm stalking you."

"Ha. Funny. Seriously though—does this have some sort of tracker or something?" I reached for the necklace, pulling my arm away from his in an attempt to take it off.

"Don't," he exclaimed, putting his hand over mine and pressing it against my chest. "You need to keep it on. It doesn't have a tracker, I promise."

"Then how did you know I was out here? You're supposed to be in class," I countered, sliding my hand away from his.

He left his palm flat on my chest for an extra beat, and in that moment, I swear every worry I ever had in my *life* disappeared. My body and mind were at total peace. Until he let go, then it all came flooding back.

"Do that again," I whispered so softly, I wasn't even sure if I actually said anything.

Xavier's chest heaved as he looked up from his hands to my face. He shook his head in the slightest of shakes, then took a step away from me.

"Soon, Cecilia. Soon." There he went again, saying my name and making me feel all sorts of things. Was it the accent? It had to be the accent...

"I need answers, Xavier."

"Meet me at the café again tonight, at five. I might have some answers for you then."

I nodded, agreeing, because what else could I do? I wanted someone to explain everything that was going on, and he was one of the three people that could do that. I wouldn't turn him down.

Xavier turned to walk away, to be swallowed into a throng of students, when at the last second, he looked back and said, "Cecilia... stay away from Ezra. Please."

He didn't say anything else before vanishing out of sight.

Seriously? What was up with people telling me to stay away from other people these days? Without any sort of explanation at that?

Then again, that was two people against Ezra now... and I still had no idea why.

Chapter 9

"CC!"

Before I could look, a hand wrapped around my wrist and pulled me through the doorway next to me. the lights were off, the door slammed behind me, and I let out a shriek worthy of a horror film.

Not only from the darkness. Not only from the abrupt movement. But also because my wrist *burned*.

"I really need to talk to you. I need to tell you something important," Ezra's voice floated to me in the dark.

I scrunched my face and lifted my hand.

Snap snap.

The room was filled with light instantly, and I beamed right along with it.

"Stop!" Ezra said, turning to face me. "You can't do any more magic!"

"Why? I'm actually getting pretty good at it. Let me tell you about Chemistry—"

But he shook his head so hard, his glasses almost flew off his face. "No! CC this is what I've been trying to tell you. I did more research the other day, and it's not good."

I placed my hands on my hips and stared him down. "Why don't you just *say* what it is you found instead of being so cryptic and vague?"

He stood straight, took a deep breath, and frowned. "This is not what I wanted to talk about," he said with a sigh, like I was frustrating him. "But fine. Like I told you before, it seems like your circle has ended."

"Except I'm here and I can snap."

Ezra sighed and pinched the bridge of his nose. "Yes, we've established that. Here's what I found though—if you don't have a mentor, or as it's called, a guide, and learn to use your magic *correctly*, then it'll build up inside of you until..."

The trailing off at the end was what panicked me. whatever it was, he didn't want to say. Which meant it was bad. Probably as bad as what I had assumed with Xavier earlier.

"What? Until what? Until I explode?"

Ezra tucked his lips in and bobbled his head side to side. "Sort of. It hasn't happened in generations upon generations, because the circles were always thriving. But when a circle dies out, when there is no one left, then occasionally a witch without a guide becomes so powerful, she... yeah. Kinda like explodes. Basically the magic will overpower her."

My heart stopped beating then. I should have collapsed to the floor. Fainted. Passed out.

Maybe lose three hours that I'm pretty sure Xavier stole, and didn't want to give back yet.

In any *normal* world, I would have had an extreme reaction. But with everything that had happened in the last week or so, it almost didn't faze me anymore.

"Okay, so where do I find a... guide?" I asked, trying to re-member the name he said.

That's when his face fell. "You can't. It has to be someone from your circle, and I can't find anyone alive. Not except..."

He didn't have to finish that sentence for me. I already knew.

"My mother."

Nodding slowly, he reached for my hand, but I jerked it away at the last second, already feeling the singe. "Is this why you said you don't think she left on her own? You said you didn't think she was dead, but her leaving couldn't have been for no reason."

Ezra stared at my hands pulled away from his and nodded. "Yeah. I think... Well, I think either someone took her, or she left to keep you safe."

"And now? Is there a way to find her so I don't freaking *explode*?"

He glanced up and caught my eye. "That I don't know."

"Great. Any other amazing news you have for me while we're trapped in a closet?"

"Yes," he rushed, almost panicked like. "Well first, I want to know why you keep pulling away from me. And what *that* is." He pointed to my neck. I instinctively the necklace, now warm to the touch and growing hotter by the second.

"It's just something I found in a drawer at home."

"Hmm," Ezra hummed, obviously not believing me. "Fine. One last thing though—Xavier."

"What about him?"

"You can't trust him, CC. I've been trying to do some digging and I'm coming up short. It's like he appeared out of nowhere. And I'm starting to think it's not a coincidence that he showed up right around the same time you learned to snap."

I huffed. Two boys both telling me not to trust the other. That was rich. "I've known how to snap since I was five, thanks."

Another sigh, another closing of his eyes. "You know what I mean, CC. You have to be careful. Don't tell him anything. Don't snap in front of him. I'm starting to think..."

This time, I wasn't clued in on what he wanted to say.

"Keep going. Don't stop on my account."

"I think he might be here to harm you." His face was so serious right now, I wouldn't have believed him otherwise.

My jaw dropped. "Xavier? Here to hurt me? If he was... Why would he ask me on a date?"

Ezra sneered like he smelled something bad. "Cecilia, I'm not sure what his deal is, but his timing doesn't seem accidental. Or that no one knows anything about him. *And* that he wants to get you *alone* every chance he can."

My head started to spin then. I couldn't keep track of who didn't like who and who had a vendetta against who and who else thought the other was out to hurt me.

If Xavier was against me, why would he give me a necklace and tell me it was to protect me? Why would he take my pain *away* at every chance he could?

Then again... why had he taken the memories away in the first place? Why did he say he was stalking me?

Once more, why did Ezra burn my skin every time he touched me?

Ezra was my best friend. Xavier was new.

Ezra's touch harmed me. Xavier's healed me.

Ezra told me to stay away from Xavier. Xavier and Gramps both told me to steer clear of Ezra.

All of this was becoming more and more muddled, with me stuck in the middle.

Taking a deep breath, I raised my hand and snapped twice, turning off the lights and strolling out of the closet with Ezra, sighing, close on my heels.

"CC, the last thing," Ezra blurted out, but I didn't look back. "I wanted to tell you I lo--"

The second I stepped into the hall, a shiver ran down my spine. I whipped my head to the right and found the cause. My sudden movement cut Ezra off.

Xavier stood at the end of the hallway, his muscular arms crossed over his chest, his eyes boring holes into me. His whole body went rigid, his jaw tensing when he saw who came out of the closet behind me.

Ezra followed my gaze, saw Xavier, then turned to me, a frown settling on his lips. "Watch yourself, CC. Be smart."

Then he fled. Ezra ran the other way right as Xavier took a step in our direction.

I stood there, helpless, slack jawed, and confused.

CHAPTER 10

By five o'clock, I wanted nothing to do with anyone in my life besides Miranda and Matt. Both of them walked me home today and avoided talking about anything Ezra or Xavier related at my request.

At first, it shocked them. Obviously. Especially the Ezra part. Matt opened his mouth once to say something, but a swift kick from Miranda stopped that.

As soon as I got home, I invited them in, but they declined. Miranda had to get ready for a play rehearsal and Matt needed to pick his brother up from his indoor soccer league practice.

Gramps wasn't home, which worried me. He had been leaving more and more lately, ever since my first snaps opened the front door. Soon, I vowed to sit him down and question him just like I planned on doing with Xavier tonight.

After I begged mercifully for my memories back.

It was the waiting around that killed me. My hand kept flying to the necklace, making sure it was still there while also wanting to rip it off and chuck it across the room.

Xavier said it wasn't a tracker. But how had he known where I was twice now? He had been waiting for me when I got out of that closet, I just knew it.

I paced around my bedroom, considering changing my outfit, doing my hair, chopping off my hair, switching shoes, and a million more things when finally it was time to go. The walk to the café would take less than ten minutes and I wanted to be early, hopefully beating him this time.

But I didn't. Xavier hadn't even gone inside, but I still showed up after him.

"Let's go," he said as soon as he saw me walk up.

"Go where?"

"Do you have the necklace on?" he asked, ignoring my question, and grabbing my hand, pulling me down the street after him.

"Yes. Why? Go where? Do what? Xavier, I really wanted—"

"In. Due. Time. Cecilia. Right now, we have somewhere to be."

I fell silent as he continued to drag me behind him, his long strides outdoing my short ones. Soon enough, we were back where we were the other day—in front of the cemetery.

"Did you know—"

"Yes."

I cocked my head. "You don't even know what I was about to say."

Instead of letting my hand go, Xavier turned to face me, picking up my other hand in his. "I do know, Cecilia Chevalier. The day you received your magic, you opened this cemetery gate. But upon further inspection, it looked completely closed. Yet, when you went home after, you opened the front door, despite having closed it. With that door, you had to close it again, unlike this gate."

My heart fell into my stomach. "What are you saying?"

"Why was this gate chained and locked, Cecilia?"

Right then, I didn't even care. All I wanted was to hear him say my name over and over and over again. It pulled me to him, made me grip his hands tighter despite the cold.

"Because it was Halloween. They always lock it on Halloween so no one goes inside and causes trouble."

"So no one..."

"Goes inside."

His black eyes bore into me, staring into the depths of my soul like he was trying to pull another answer out.

"So no one... gets out?" I mouthed, unable to tear my gaze away from him. From his high cheekbones. His thin, pale lips. From the white streak in his otherwise shadowy hair. To his tall stature, his broad shoulders, his icy cold hands, his long legs.

To his jeans. His black sneakers. This sidewalk.

Sidewalk. Shoes. Jeans.

"You kidnapped me," I whispered, as a flood of memories came back to me all in a rush. This sidewalk. His shoes. The cemetery gates opening. Me, staring at his lower half and the sidewalk, hauled over his shoulder until I woke up. Then, he cradled me in his arms, staring down at me as I looked up at him.

This time, though, remembering it all didn't make my head didn't hurt.

"You got out," I whispered low. He nodded slowly, capturing my gaze with his again. "You got out."

"We've been waiting for you for eighteen years, Cecilia. Eighteen years. Then, you called to us. You brought us here. You were nothing like I expected, but you are the reason we're here."

I shook my head, blinking back tears I didn't understand why I had. "What are you saying? What happened in those three hours, Xavier? Who... Who are you?"

"It's easier if I show you. I'm sorry. It'll be painful." He lifted a hand to my cheek, brushing it with the back of his forefinger, tapping on my temple. "I'll do my best to help you, but promise me, do *not* take that necklace off."

"I won't take the necklace off," I repeated, somewhat on autopilot. Either I completely trusted him or I was in some sort of trance, but whatever was going on, I went with.

Xavier lifted his hand and the cemetery gate opened for us. I gasped, my jaw dropped. "You're a witch too?"

He shook his hair, the charcoal strands not moving an inch. "No, Cecilia. Think. Before we can go in, I need you to understand."

"You... just did that," I gestured to the open gate. "And... you were called to me? When I opened the gate?"

Xavier nodded slowly, his face unchanging.

"I called you... and you were in the cemetery... but the gate was closed. I opened it, but it was closed."

"We couldn't risk you coming inside. Not before you understood. Not before... not before we were sure."

"So you closed it. Whoever... Whoever you are with closed it? But how, I didn't see anyone around." Not that I had really been paying attention...

"You wouldn't have seen us."

"Why, you're good at playing hide and seek? Xavier, I'm so *tired* of this! the vagueness, the runaround, the hiding of the truth. All I want are my memories back and some straight answers."

"I know. I'm sorry, Cecilia. But before we go in, you have to understand. *You* have to figure it out."

"What is it I'm supposed to be figuring out?" If I were younger, I would have stomped my foot in frustration. There was so much swarming through my mind right now, I couldn't keep *anything* straight. All I wanted to do was snap my fingers and send myself home, tucked into bed, with some chocolate.

Actually...

I lifted my hand, but Xavier's own flashed out and grabbed it before I could do anything.

"No," he bit, "not here. Not now. Cecilia, *think*. Please, we don't have much time." He glanced around behind us, then back through the gates he had opened.

What was stopping me from just walking through? Besides Xavier clutching to me like I was a life preserver, and he was drowning.

"Okay! Figure this out. Figure out how you got here right after I discovered my magic. Figure out how I opened the gate, called to you, and somehow you, or whoever you're talking about, closed it before I could do anything else. Figure out why your hands are always cold, why you have a white streak in your hair. Figure out how you kidnapped me, took me here to this cemetery, stole my memories, and deposited me back in the nurse's office three hours later. Figure out why you want me to stay away from Ezra. Figure out why you can somehow heal my migraines with the touch... of... your... fingers. Figure out... why this necklace... heats up... Why you said it would... protect me..." I slowed down at the end, starting to put puzzle pieces together.

Ezra said I needed a guide. He said my circle had been wiped out, that no one was left to teach me except my mother.

Xavier said he had been searching for me for eighteen years. But *how* would he have known to search for me unless...

My gaze flicked up to meet his. He stared at me expectedly, his eyes slightly softer now.

"You know my mother."

Chapter 11

"Yes. I do. Well, we do. I never met her. Keep going Cecilia. Think of the gates. Please, *think*."

"I opened the gates. You closed them. Faster than I could have ever seen you do, chain and lock and all. Now, you just opened them with a wave of your hands, but you said you're not a witch. Who else would be able to do that?"

Xavier nodded, still glancing through the gates like we were running out of time.

It finally hit me. What I had asked Ezra from the start—if there are such things as witches...

"Why not vampires and aliens?" I whispered, my eyes widening as I turned toward Xavier. "If there're witches, why not vampires and aliens. All fictional stories are rooted in some sort of history, Ezra said."

Xavier locked his eyes on mine, a slow, sly smile growing on his lips. His brilliant white teeth gleamed in the now almost completely set sun, brighter than they should have.

"Vampires... and aliens..." I muttered, staring at his mouth. Just as the words left my lips, two sharp canine teeth descended, becoming larger than the rest of his teeth.

"Cecilia, I need you to say it," Xavier pleaded, squeezing my hands and returning my attention back to him.

"Vampires. You're... you're a *vampire*."

Instead of nodding, he let out a huge sigh of relief, like he was *glad*.

Glad? How could he be *happy* about this? Right in front of me stood a living, breathing, *vampire*. A soulless creature who wanted to suck my blood and leave me for dead.

I tried to pry my hands away from him, but he held tight, his head turning back to look at the cemetery.

"Let me go!" I stuttered, still trying to yank my hands from his grip. He barely blinked in my direction as he was too focused on what was beyond the gates.

The gates I absolutely did *not* want to go through right now. Whatever was back there I had no interest in.

Ezra was right. I should have listened. I should have stayed far, far away from Xavier. This whole time he was luring me here. It was all a trap. He had already kidnapped me once, stole the memories, and made me live in a constant state of struggle for days. That was probably only the beginning.

"Xavier, let me go! I promise, I won't tell anyone, just please, let me go." I tried to hide the pleading in my voice, pushing back the sob that wanted to escape.

Vampires. I had said it as a joke to Ezra, but it had been the truth. Witches. Vampires. They were all real.

"What do you want from me? What are you going to do with me?" My whole body started shaking, from my hands down to my toes.

That must have gotten Xavier's attention, because he finally looked back at me. He saw the terror on my face and dropped my hands immediately.

"Do with you? What are you talking about?"

But I didn't stick around to answer his question. The second he let go of my hands, I turned and bolted, running down the sidewalk so fast everything seemed to be in a blur.

Tears streamed down my face, the wind whipping my hair back as I ran.

How could I have been so stupid? From the first moment I saw him, I knew something seemed off. Ezra clocked it right away, too, warning me about it multiple times.

I fell for the defined cheekbones, the British accent, the smooth moves, and the unquestionable way he said my name, like nothing else mattered in the world.

It was all an elaborate ruse, a giant trap, and I was the idiot who stepped right in.

My lungs burned as I kept going, the necklace lifting up and hitting my chest with every step. I reached up and yanked it over my head. Part of me wanted to toss it in the nearest bush and forget about it, but I shoved it into my pocket instead.

There was only one thing I could think of doing right now, one person I could trust, one place I needed to be.

I knew he would be home, and I knew exactly where to find him. Even though his mother didn't want him around me, the lack of her car in the driveway told me I had some time.

Tiptoeing around the side of the house, I made it under his window. With no rocks around to toss, and sort of scared I'd break the window even if I did have some, I did the next best thing.

Snap snap.

Ezra's window slid open and a gust of wind blew his curtains inside. It was enough to get his attention, to bring him to the window and look out.

One glance at my tear-streaked face was all he needed. In less than a minute, he was downstairs, in the backyard, his arms around me.

We stood like that, my tears ruining his shirt, his arms tightening with every sob I let out, for a solid five minutes before he ushered me down the small slope toward the swing set.

"CC... what happened?" he said softly as we both sat down and started rocking back and forth.

"I was stupid, Ez. I fell for it."

His head snapped up, looking directly at me. "Fell for what?"

"Xavier's trap."

He leapt to his feet then, taking one step over, then crouching in front of me. He held my hands and made sure I was looking directly at him. "What trap? What happened?"

I started to speak, but he stopped me.

"Wait. CC, I'm holding your hands."

With a sniffle, I nodded. "And?"

"I haven't been able to touch you. What changed?" There was hopefulness in his tone.

My shoulders sank as I leaned into the chain on the swing. "I don't know. But Ezra, you were right."

"I was?" he squeaked out quickly. Then he composed himself a bit more. "I mean, I was. Exactly what was I right about?"

"Xavier. You told me not to trust him. You were right, he's—" I cut myself off as a cool breeze washed over me, sending a profound shiver down my spine.

The same kind of shiver I got when Xavier was around.

"I... I can't say," I continued, swiveling my head around to see where he was. He had to be close, that was for sure. Was he listening? Watching? Was it the necklace again, some sort of tracker he claimed it wasn't?

Or was it his *vampire* senses? He said using my magic called him, and yet I just snapped to get Ezra's attention. That was so dumb of me.

"I can't use my magic," I whispered.

"I told you not to," Ezra replied, the wrinkles between his brows deepening. "You don't have a guide. All of your magic will build up if you don't know how to use—"

"No, I mean I can't use it because of *him*. He'll find me. And I think... I think he wants to kill me."

CHAPTER 12

Ezra's hands on mine tightened as he stood, pulled me off the swing, and back into his arms again. It was comforting, as Ezra always was for me, but for some reason it didn't feel the same.

It didn't feel the way it did when Xavier said my name. When he laid his cold hand over my chest, looking into my eyes.

Ezra's hug felt... emptier than normal. I knew he wanted to help, to figure out this Xavier problem, but... something felt off.

"Ezra? What do we do?"

He rubbed his hand up and down my back. "We'll figure it out, CC. I promise. I won't let him hurt you."

I sighed. If Xavier wanted to hurt me, wouldn't he have done it by now?

"He's the reason behind those missing hours the other day, when I passed out. It wasn't because of the water—" I stumbled back, clutching at my head. The intense pain returned just as soon as I tried to remember what happened after the water fountain.

The only difference now was that Xavier wasn't here to take the pain away. At least, he wasn't coming out of the shadows to help.

I stood up straight, rubbing at my head, trying to move past the pain and past the memory.

"CC?" Ezra said, resting his hands on my shoulders. "You're my best friend. I won't let anything happen to you. Tell me what happened before you came here. What trap did he set? Where did he take you?"

I shook my head, not wanting to talk about Xavier anymore. "I can't," I said, not telling him I was for some reason physically unable to make the word *vampire* come out of my mouth. That was no doubt Xavier's doing. "I just... I need answers, Ezra. I got more than I wanted from Xavier, but I need to know about the circles. The reason Sonya left. Most importantly, what happened to my mom. This has all been so crazy and I feel like my entire life is imploding and I can't even talk to anyone about it, and your mom took you away and—"

Ezra cut me off, but not by saying something.

By *kissing* me.

He slid the hands on my shoulders up my neck, letting one cradle the back of my head and the other firmly on the side of my jaw. His lips were on mine, pressing into me as he held me steady.

Ezra was *kissing me*. I blinked, unmoving as I tried to take this in.

I'd kissed other guys before. While those kisses were all decent, nothing overly spectacular, this one was different. By all means, there should have been fireworks, parades, explosions, and the feeling of uncontrollable love coming from somewhere deep inside of me.

But there wasn't.

The kiss was fine. Ezra, surprisingly, was a good kisser. It wasn't something I had ever thought about him being, but he was. However, I didn't even feel the smallest of a spark.

I didn't hate the kiss. I sort of hated that it came from Ezra, though.

"CC? Is this... is this okay?" he whispered after pulling back an inch and resting his head on mine.

"I... I don't know," I replied honestly. That dang shiver ran down my spine again, and for some reason, a wave of anger with it. But it wasn't *my* anger.

Xavier was definitely here. And he was pissed.

"I'm sorry to just spring this on you like this… but CC, you have to know. I've been in love with you for years."

My heart stopped beating at that admission. I stumbled backwards, the back of my legs hitting the swing. Ezra reached out to grab my arm, but at the last second, a rush of wind pushed me into the swing seat, saving me from falling over.

"You're… you're what?" I stuttered, still in shock at what he said. That was twice now that someone dropped a bomb on me, expecting me to just take it all in at face value.

Ezra sat on the swing next to me again. "I'm in love with you, CC. Have been for a while. I wanted to tell you a while ago, but then everything with your magic, the research, and everything got so crazy for a while."

My lips flapped open and shut a few times, not sure what to say. Should I say I love you back? I mean, I did, but I wasn't sure it was in the same way he loved me.

Ezra had been my best friend for most of my life, always there for me, always sticking by my side.

But this? This I never saw coming. I thought we had beaten the statistic that said guys and girls couldn't be best friends. We shared everything with each other, yet he had been hiding this from me?

"I… I don't know what to say, Ezra."

"You don't—" he stopped when he saw headlights flash across the driveway. "Crap. Mom's home. You gotta go, CC. We'll talk tomorrow, okay?"

He jumped up and pulled me to my feet again, turning and pushing me toward my house. "Remember, in the meantime, *no snapping.*"

I sprinted across the two backyards and to my house without another word. As soon as I reached my room, I dug into my jeans pocket and grabbed the necklace. I opened my window and chucked it outside.

I had no idea if Xavier was still watching, still waiting in the shadows or not. But if so, then great. He could have that ridiculous thing back. I didn't want it anymore. I didn't want anything to do with him.

There was so much to soak in from tonight, I didn't even know where to start. So instead of dealing with my issues, I did the next best thing:

I went to sleep.

The sun woke me up early the next morning, which was great because I hadn't set my alarm for school.

The delicious scent of coffee brewing downstairs hit me as I hopped around trying to get my jeans on. They were the same pair as yesterday, but who really cared. I threw on a different sweater, tossed my hair into the quickest braid of my life and ran downstairs.

"I'm late! I'm on time, but I'm also late," I shouted to Gramps wherever he was. It was something he always said that I had somehow picked up over the years. It meant we weren't really late, but if we didn't keep moving, we would be late.

So I kept moving. I danced around the kitchen island, grabbing a mug with the phrase 'world's okayest grandpa' on it, filled it just shy of the brim, then snatched a plain bagel off the counter. It would have to be a cream cheese-less day, which would definitely put a damper on my mood.

"Come back straight after school today, Cecilia!" Gramps called just before I shut the door. I didn't have time to question him, but also didn't have anywhere else I wanted to be. Home was fine. Home was safe.

Home was void of vampires and best friends-turned-more and magical mishaps and chaos. Which was what my life had dove into being lately.

Ezra didn't catch up with me again today, which meant his mom drove him. She really was playing into this 'stay away from CC' card hard.

I only stopped moving when I got to my locker, needing to empty my backpack and grab a few other books before class.

I half expected to see Ezra waiting there, or even Xavier, but was met with glorious silence.

It didn't last long, though, before Matt and Miranda came around the corner. I really couldn't deal with them right now, so I swiped my phone from my pocket and held it up to my ear, having an imaginary conversation with Gramps.

"Yeah. I know, Gramps. Yup. Hold on one sec." I moved the phone away from my mouth and whispered to my friends, "I gotta talk to Gramps for a few, but meet you later? See you in Chem, Matt."

They both nodded, but looked at me strangely. Sure, I didn't like talking on the phone, but with the excuse that it was Gramps, I could get away with it for now.

If I were braver, I would just *snap snap* and divert their attention away, but knowing that using magic possibly both called Xavier to me and could potentially make me blow up soon, I didn't give it a whirl.

Once out of sight, I put the phone down and crouched to take books out of my backpack. That's when I froze, almost falling over onto the ground.

My headphones were in my backpack. The ones that had disappeared after my three-hour kidnapping.

But that wasn't all.

Wrapped around the headphones was the necklace I had thrown out of my bedroom window last night, with a note attached.

Keep this on for your protection.

CHAPTER 13

I couldn't help myself. By the time I got to class, I was a nervous wreck. I couldn't focus, I couldn't sit still, I could barely see straight.

After the bell rang, dismissing first period, I stumbled my way to the nurse's office. Knowing that Xavier had not only been watching, but had been in my bedroom after I went to sleep threw me into a frenzy I didn't know how to handle. I needed to go home and collect myself.

So when I got to Nurse Paige's office, I had to do what needed to be done.

Snap snap.

"Nurse Paige, I need an excuse form to go home. I'm not feeling well."

She barely looked up before grabbing a notepad from her right and scribbling some words on it. "Of course, darling. I hope you feel better. I'll put it into the system right away."

"Thank you." I took the note and headed for the front doors, showing it to the security guard to be allowed out.

The quickest way home would be past the cemetery again. Every cell in my body screamed at me to take another way, but doing so would add a good fifteen minutes to my five-minute walk. If I went so far out of my way, I didn't know if I would make it home without throwing up or passing out.

So I put on the bravest face I could and took off.

The second I passed the gates, I felt the gurgle in my stomach. I couldn't look at them without thinking of Xavier, of last night, of what he was.

Vampire.

What laid beyond those gates? What was back there that he was trying to bring me into? What would have happened if—

"CC?"

I stopped. I would have rather stopped *anywhere* but here, in front of the gates. But the voice belonged to someone who shouldn't have been here.

Ezra.

"What are you doing here?" he asked, coming out from behind a tree a few feet in front of me.

I frowned. "Me? What about you? Why are you not in class? Your mom—"

He waved his hand, and that's when I noticed something. A ring. Ezra had a ring on his pinky. He never wore rings before to my knowledge. I definitely didn't notice one last night when his hands were all over me.

"My mom knows exactly where I am and what I'm doing."

My blood froze. Ezra's voice had lowered, his eyes narrowing as he looked at me. It wasn't comforting or in any way protective.

"What are you doing?"

"You wanted me to tell you more about the circle, right?" he said, coming closer now. My pulse quickened as he got closer, but he didn't stop moving. He circled around me, looking at me up and down like I was a snack and he was ravenous. "About Sonya?"

"Sure, but it can wait. I was going home. Not feeling good and—"

"Sonya married into our family. It was your family that started everything." Ezra's voice sent a chill straight to the bone. "They said we kidnapped her."

Kidnapped. This took a turn I wasn't expecting.

"When Sonya left, your circle declared us enemies."

"Us?" Where did the talk about 'us' come from? Everything he mentioned before was about his ancestors, the research, the line that stopped forty years ago.

I desperately wanted to keep moving, away from the cemetery at least. But Ezra stepped in front of me, blocking my exit.

"They wanted Sonya back. Because she was *powerful*. One of the most powerful. Losing her weakened their circle. And they had been at war ever since."

"War? What? What does any of this have to do with me? With you?"

The low, guttural laugh from Ezra didn't bring happiness to my heart like it used to. This laugh was different. It was sinister. He kept circling me, getting closer and closer each time. "You once asked why only girls were witches. Well, turns out, they use the men for protection."

I was truly, deeply terrified now. The guy in front of me looked and sounded nothing like my best friend. "Ezra, what is going on? What are you doing? Is this about yesterday—"

"Yesterday proved to me that you'll never love me the way I love you. And it showed me how superior you think you are because of your little *snaps*," Ezra spat out, his lip curling into a snarl.

"*What*? Ez, we barely had time to discuss—"

"Enough."

My lips clamped shut, my eyes wide in fear. All I wanted was to go home, dive under the covers, and pretend this never happened. To go back in time to Halloween and somehow prevent myself from ever snapping my fingers again.

This wasn't a blessing I had been bestowed upon. It was a curse.

"Our circles have been at war, CC. For centuries. One we thought we had been victorious in. Until *you*. We were on top, finally dismantling your circle. But no... you had to come along. And now you need to be dealt with."

No matter where I tried to step, Ezra was there, leaning in close, being all up in my business. I wondered if I could snap him backwards, somehow bind him to that tree he had been lurking behind.

"What are you talking about, Ezra? War? Dismantling? What does it mean? I—what are you doing?" I cried out as he took one more step closer to me, his hand reaching out to grab mine, to stop me from snapping. He didn't get a chance before I yanked it away. Necklace or not, he wasn't going to hurt me.

"You said you loved me, Ezra," I pleaded with him. The guy in front of me was *not* the same guy who comforted me last night. Not the same one who helped with my homework. The same guy who had movie marathons, walked with me to school, shared his ice cream when mine fell on the ground.

Ezra said he loved me. He *kissed* me. He was my best friend and now... Now he was...

"He's a hunter, Cecilia. He's here to take your magic." Xavier's voice should have scared me, but it didn't. Saying my name still brought a sense of peace to me, even though I wasn't sure why. Literally nothing else was bringing me peace.

I was stuck between a vampire and a hunter.

Whatever that was. Not a single part of me wanted to stick around and find out. If the boys wanted to fight about it, then I'd gladly let them. As long as I could get the heck out of here.

Ezra had dropped his hand the second Xavier spoke up. I had no idea how long Xavier had been watching, listening, but if it was anything like last night, he could have been here the entire time.

"My magic? Speaking of, does anyone know if a little snap snap can make me go *poof* right about now? I'm so down to try—"

"Cecilia," Xavier interrupted my rant. How rude of him. A creaking noise settled to my right, and I glanced over my shoulder, finding that dang gate slowly inching open. It wasn't as grand of a gesture as last night, or as openly wide, only big enough for one person to squeeze through at a time.

That had to be on purpose. What the purpose was, shockingly, I didn't know. There wasn't a whole lot I did know, and I was really, really getting tired of that.

"Ezra is exactly what I thought he was. A hunter."

"And you are exactly what I figured you to be, *vampire*."

My jaw dropped, my gaze ping-ponging between the two guys standing in front and behind me. Ezra knew about Xavier? And Xavier knew about Ezra? *I* didn't even know whatever this was Ezra was supposed to be.

Why was I always the last to know things?

I raised my hand a little. Xavier's hand shot out to grab my wrist, but I yanked it away. I didn't need *anyone* touching me at this time. Besides, I wasn't going to snap. I just had a question. Or fifty. "Excuse me, I would just like to ask—what is a hunter and why is it bad that Ezra is one?"

The question seemed as stupid as I thought it did the second it left my mouth. Ezra smirked, crossing his arms over his chest. Seemingly overnight, his puny, muscle free arms somehow bulked up.

That scared me more than the look on his face.

"He's here to take your magic. Certain male members of magical circle families are deemed hunters. They are set to destroy other witches and circles in order to keep their circle safe or more powerful," Xavier explained in a low voice. I looked to my side, finding him standing in a somewhat defensive pose, his hands fisted at his side, leaning forward slightly, his lips twitching.

I remembered his teeth from last night, the pearly white gleaming in the late sun, the canines descending through his gums.

"*My* magic? The same magic he's told me not to use or I'll explode?"

Ezra huffed, and a proud look crossed his face. Xavier finally took a step forward, but not too close. Just enough to be slightly in front of me. If he took another step to the side, he'd be shielding me with his body, but right now he was still a good few feet away from Ezra at this point.

"He tricked you, Cecilia. He wants your magic to build up to the point where you cannot control it. It makes it easier for him to take."

"Your magic and your mothers," Ezra said haughtily. "We haven't found her yet—"

"And you never will," Xavier interrupted, his chest heaving now.

"But once we get yours, it'll be fine," Ezra finished, staring at me.

"Ezra... you're my best friend. Why are you doing this? Why would you take my magic? You just told me you loved me and—"

"The circle and the family come first. My mother showed me that last night. It's not personal, CC. It's family."

It's not personal? Did he really just say that? The guy who just did a complete one-eighty on me in less than twenty-four hours said it's not *personal*?

I thought of something just then. "I thought you said records for your family stopped forty years ago. How did your mother—"

"Only because they wiped the records," Ezra interrupted. I *really* wished he would stop doing that. It was incredibly rude, not to mention slightly demeaning. "They moved to DeBruin to keep an eye on your grandmother when she was pregnant. If it was a boy, they knew the line would end. There hadn't been a hunter born in your family in a hundred years. If your mother had been a boy, none of this would be happening."

"But her mother existed," Xavier said through gritted teeth, "and you kept going after them anyway."

Ezra shrugged like it wasn't a big deal. To me, it was. At least, it should have been. But I still didn't understand.

"So your family, your *hunters* have been searching for my mother this whole time?"

Ezra nodded. "The moment she found out she was pregnant, she fled. We lost track of her, but kept an eye on your grandmother, according to my mother. When we found out you were a girl, well, we called in reinforcements. Then, rumors of your mother being alive hit. We had assumed she was dead, a hunter from another area taking her out. Our circle is the strongest in the country, probably the world. I'm the first hunter born in a century as well."

He flashed the ring on his finger, a gold band with a grotesque skull with a crown of thorns over the top. He said it like he was proud of the fact. Proud of the fact that he was sent to kill me.

Or take my magic. Whichever came first, it seemed.

CHAPTER 19

"Cecilia," Xavier whispered. "Your mother is the last in the circle prior to you. When you were young, they realized your mother was still alive somewhere. So they took your grandmother."

Ezra let out another low laugh. "Can't have three of you in this world, can we? You'll start another war."

"You killed my grandmother?" I exclaimed. Obviously I knew it wasn't Ezra personally, but still. His family sent my mother away *and* had my grandmother killed.

"A circle starts with *three* witches. Poor old Gram took one for the team. When we found out you were your mother's daughter, and that she was still alive but on the run, we did what we had to do."

"What, you thought between me, my mother, and my grandmother, we'd kidnap some of your family members like you kidnapped Sonya?" I shot back, suddenly really, *really* pissed off at Ezra. Xavier chuckled under his breath next to me, but Ezra just puffed out his chest and glowered.

Did I know if Sonya really was kidnapped? Absolutely not. Did I know anything about Ezra's family circle? Not a dang thing. Was I even sure about anything in *my* circle? That's also a big nope.

"Your circle was *finished*. Your mother fled. Your grandmother gone. Regrettably, draining her magic at her age took her as well, but it was for the greater good. It was over. There was no one to teach you magic. By all accounts, you shouldn't have any. We made sure of it. We had all the power."

"That's why you took Sonya," I said, now connecting the dots. He said Sonya had been one of the most powerful witches of the time. Marrying someone didn't make them switch circles. They took her so *my* family circle didn't get too powerful. "And now what? Your circle is overpowering the rest. After you've eliminated my entire extended family."

"We don't kill them. Not all of them." Ezra rolled his eyes like he was explaining something to a toddler. "We just drain their powers."

I paled. "Is that what you're going to do to me? Drain my powers? Ezra, how could you? You've been my best friend for years and years. Now, overnight, you want to get rid of me?"

Xavier finally took the step to the side, shielding me from my most likely now ex- best friend. "Cecilia. Where is the necklace? You need the necklace."

Now I rolled my eyes. "Oddly enough, I found it in my backpack this morning. Did you have your fun being a creepy stalker?"

"I gave it, the headphones, and the note to your grandfather. Who invited me in. Who put it in your backpack for me. You need it on, *now*, Cecilia."

I barely blinked before Xavier flashed around to my back and a weight settled on my chest. It all happened so fast, I didn't even know what occurred until he was back in front of me, completely blocking me now.

"I knew that was you," Ezra said, also looking slightly stunned at Xavier's quickness. "When my touch burned her, I knew she had her protection."

"This...The burning. It was from this?" I grasped the medallion between my fingers, staring at it.

"It's the protection of those sworn to protect your circle. Protection against hunters."

"You knew?" I asked Ezra, even though I sort of wanted nothing to do with him right now.

"Not fully until last night, when my mother opened my eyes to everything she had been keeping from me. Once she heard your name and witch in the same sentence the other week, she knew it was time."

Xavier reached behind him and laced one hand with mine. I let him, even though I wasn't sure why. "Hunters are brutal, vicious creatures, Cecilia. They can't control themselves and most of the time they end up killing witches. That's why he wanted all your magic to build up. It would be easier for him to drain it all in one go. Usually they drain too much; they can't stop themselves. Their circle rewards them for how much magic they take and *inexperienced* hunters take *everything*."

The enunciation of the two words were like knives to my heart. Ezra was an inexperienced hunter. He literally became one overnight.

Which meant... if allowed access to me, he would drain everything.

"If I was supposed to have been protected against hunters," I said quietly, "where have you been for eighteen years?"

"As hidden as you," Ezra sneered.

Xavier looked over his shoulder at me and his look said everything I needed to know.

He had been with my mother. He said he had never met her, but his family had. "We've been blocked from you. Without your mother or grandmother, we assumed you hadn't developed your powers and therefore would be safe. But the day you did, the day you opened these gates.... It called us here."

"And last night, my mother told me the truth. When she saw you sprinting across the backyard, she said it was time I knew everything," Ezra said like he didn't want to miss any part of the conversation. "And now, I need to do my job and protect my circle. From you."

His eyes flashed red and his hands fell to his side, a sort of crackling, static-y sensation emitting from them. He took one step forward, but Xavier was there blocking me.

At the same time, the tingles in my hands returned. A gut instinct told me to start snapping wildly, to protect myself, protect my circle, protect Xavier.

But could I really do that to my best friend? Was I ready to fight him?

"Cecilia, you need to go through the gates," Xavier said, his eyes still trained on Ezra.

Ezra lunged left, then right, trying to get around Xavier. When that was no use, he threw a punch. I shrieked, but Xavier ducked and barreled into Ezra, knocking him to the ground.

"Cecilia! The cemetery! Go past the gates *now*!"

A Snap of Fate

Chapter 1

"Shh... it's okay. You're okay, darling. You're safe in here, with us."

The soft strokes pushing back my hair from my forehead to my shoulder soothed me so much, I almost didn't want to open my eyes. All of the sudden, I was small again, three years old, before Gramma died. She used to hold me in her arms, sing me a song I couldn't remember now, and stroke my hair back just like this.

"It's alright, dear. You can open your eyes whenever you want. You're safe. You're alright."

That voice... that voice sounded so familiar, yet so foreign. The accent... it was like... like...

Xavier's.

My eyes flew open, and I bolted upright, surprising the person behind me.

"Oh! Alright then, that's one way to do it."

Cold. Everything around me was cold. Marble. Granite. I didn't know the name of the stone, but the room was made of concrete and stone. All of it so... cold.

"Who are you? Where am I?" I blurted out, standing now and turning in circles to see all around me. My heart pounded behind my ribs and I broke out in a sweat.

"Cecilia Potentia Chevalier, you are perfectly safe in here. My name is Elodie, and I am here to protect you."

The way she said my name, like we were long-lost friends reuniting for the first time. Like it was familiar to her, yet I had never heard her name before in my life.

"Who are you? How do you know my name?"

Her smile fell for a second before she sighed and patted the ground next to her. She sat on a long, tufted purple cushion, where I was probably laid out a moment ago, too. "Please, sit. Let me explain what my incorrigible son obviously couldn't."

"Your son? Who's your—Xavier. You're Xavier's mother?"

Pain erupted behind my eyes again, thinking of Xavier's name. In the span of a heartbeat, long, cold fingers laid upon my temple, slightly massaging, slightly pushing into my head. A moment later, the pain disappeared, but the memories stayed.

Xavier and Ezra. Outside the cemetery. Ezra attacking Xavier. Xavier yelling for me to go through the gates.

"I went through the gates," I whispered, looking up at the beautiful woman in front of me. She had long, dark hair like Xavier, reaching all the way to her waist, with one long white streak behind her ear.

Her oval face was pale, her lips bright red, with dark eyes, also just like her son. He was a carbon copy of her.

"Yes, you did. You trusted Xavier."

I trusted him. Even though I had no idea who he really was or why a vampire wanted to help me, I trusted him. My gut told me to listen, and I did.

"You're... a *vampire*," I stated, with absolutely no confidence behind it. I was still clueless as to what that meant, but I had chosen to trust the vampire over the hunter.

The hunter. My best friend. The one who wanted to drain all of my magic for the sake of his family. The family who sent my mother into hiding and drained my grandmother enough to kill her.

"I think I'll sit down now," I muttered, suddenly feeling dizzy with all the commotion inside my head.

Elodie took my elbow and helped me. "You know, you can use your magic in here. It's safe. The hunters cannot locate you in a vampire lair."

"Why don't I just live here then?" I said it more to myself than her, but it got a low chuckle.

"You could, if you wanted. I cannot guarantee it is an exciting sort of life, living in a cemetery. Even we go outside at times."

"And if I go outside, Ezra will find—wait. Where's Xavier? What happened to him? Did Ezra get—"

Elodie laid a hand on my arm and a wave of calm washed over me. It was as if she took all my panic and worry away with one single touch. Sort of how Xavier did.

"Shhh, Cecilia. It's all alright. Xavier did a magnificent job making sure you were safe. Fortunately, Ezra is inexperienced, and when Xavier showed his abilities to overpower him, Ezra ran."

So Ezra was safe too. That fact made me glad, but didn't bring the same sense of ease as it should have. I didn't want him to be hurt, but on the other hand... he also wanted me dead.

"Is Xavier okay?"

Elodie nodded, her long hair draping over her shoulders. "He is fine. A much more experienced fighter than your friend. Nay a scratch on my son." I breathed a sigh of relief, making Elodie smile. "You've taken to Xavier."

I shrugged and looked down, picking at non-existent lint on the pillow. "He's been nice, even if he's been vague."

"All had to be revealed in due time, sweet Cecilia."

I huffed out a laugh. "That's exactly what he said. Minus the sweet part..."

"There are things you needed to understand before you could even pass through those gates. That is why we had to close them when you opened them. How odd it was, to receive the call, flash here as fast as we could, and then see you heading toward the gates. Had you gone through them without knowing of your protectors, all would be lost."

I frowned. "All would be lost?"

Elodie shifted, tucking her feet behind her, and looking at me, her dark eyes serious, yet peaceful. "Yes, sweet Cecilia. Had you gone through the gates without knowing of the vampires sworn to protect your family circle, it could be disastrous to your magic. You wouldn't be able to pass through the wall of protection, and we wouldn't be able to welcome you in."

"I'm sorry," I whispered, an overwhelming feeling of sadness coming over me. "I really don't understand. None of this makes sense."

"It is not your fault, child. You do not have a guide. I cannot imagine the questions you must have. Let me explain just a little, then we'll get you to Xavier, alright?"

She reached over and took my hands in hers, one of her thumbs brushing over the back of my knuckles. "Vampires are not as you see them in the fictional world. Not all of them, at least. Our specific subset of vampires are sworn protectors of the witches. Long, long, long ago, much before you can imagine, vampires were hunted almost to extinction. So badly, that we had to turn to the one group we were most afraid of in order to seek help."

"The witches," I breathed, completely captivated by the way her storytelling.

"Yes. Vampires and witches stayed apart until then, as the vampires had been afraid of their powers, afraid to cross them. But then, a deal was struck. The witches would help the vampires from being hunted if they did the same for the witches. Circle hunters had gotten out of control at that point, destroying circles everywhere, almost as badly as the vampires were being hunted."

"A win-win deal."

Elodie nodded. "As you can see, we are still keeping our end of the deal. The witches were capable and powerful. And it may have helped that all those fiction stories were created, and we vampires became more feared."

A smile twitched on my lips. Ezra had said all fiction had been based in reality at some point. It seemed like the stories got twisted, but that didn't matter now.

"So vampires are not soulless creatures of the night. They're protectors of witches."

Elodie rolled her eyes. "Yes. We can also go out during the day and not burn up. That was granted by the witches generations ago. The sun does not harm our subset of vampires, the protectors."

"And you couldn't protect me because you didn't know about me." That I stated as a fact, getting as much from Xavier's explanation.

"Correct. Without a guide, your magic was undetected until it manifested. Your mother—"

"You know my mother?" I interrupted, not even feeling bad about it.

Elodie nodded again. "Yes, I do. Very well. She is one of my best friends, and I have been her protector since her magic developed."

Her protector. Elodie was Mom's protector and Xavier was mine. "Then... why aren't you with her?" If she was alone and in hiding, she could be found. She could—

"She is safe. After Xavier was called here the night your magic appeared, I spoke with her. She wants me here, dear Cecilia. With you. Protecting you. She loves you, Cecilia, more than you can ever know."

CHAPTER 2

I leaned back against the cold stone slab behind me. My head swam, knowing not only that Mom was alive, but she was okay. She had been protected.

By vampires.

"Mother?" A familiar voice filled the quiet chamber.

"Xavier, there you are. Please, come. I'll leave you two to talk awhile. Then, Cecilia, we must be going."

"Going?" I gasped, struggling to stand. "Going where?"

Xavier flashed to me, appearing toe to toe before I drew my next breath. "Sit, Cecilia. Please. Now that you understand, I can help."

I did as he asked, shuffling over so he could join me. The massive stone door opened and closed across the room as Elodie left.

"I like your mom," I whispered, closing my eyes and turning my head so my cheek could lean against the cool stone.

"She's okay as far as mom's go," Xavier answered. "Now, do you want all your memories back? It might be painful..."

Without opening my eyes, I nodded.

"I'm sorry, Cecilia," he whispered softly as he laid his hands on my face, his icy fingers pressing on my temples.

I winced as my head erupted again, but the pain didn't last long. Xavier left his hands on my head an extra beat after it had subsided, trailing down my cheeks before pulling them away.

"Please. I can answer anything you may ask now."

"So this is due time, huh?" I tried to joke, but it fell a little flat. I peeked one eye open, though, finding Xavier with a half smile on his face.

I liked seeing him smile. Seeing him happy.

"You're my protector," I said, more of a statement than a question.

"That was an easy one to figure out, I feel," he answered. "Thank you for leaving the necklace on."

"You brought me here. To this chamber." I wasn't talking about tonight, though. This was the missing three hours from the other week. The memory came back easily and without any discomfort in my head. "You touched me in the hallway after the water fountain and I passed out."

Xavier nodded, not a strand of his perfect hair falling out of place. "Something between us... I didn't know exactly what happened. Why you fainted at my touch. But, admittedly, I took advantage of it. Unconscious, and with me, you could pass through the gates. We had to be sure you were who we thought you were. We didn't think you would develop any magic without a guide in your life. Most wouldn't."

The way he said 'most' made me pause. But I was done with vague, with no answers. "What do you mean, most wouldn't?"

That brought out a full smile, like he was proud of me for catching on. He grinned, spreading his cheeks and showing his elongated canines. Instead of being afraid of them, though, I was intrigued. Pulled toward him.

"It takes a special kind of witch to develop powers without being exposed to them during her lifetime. It's one thing to be surrounded by witches and learning from a young age. To be completely in the dark, yet still pull from the reserves you didn't know you had? You're special, Cecilia. And most likely powerful."

My eyes went wide. "Powerful? Me? The girl who makes water fountains explode?"

Xavier laughed and reached for my hand. "Yes, you, Cecilia. That is why Ezra's abilities manifested so quickly too. I don't doubt his mother realized what had happened and figured out exactly what we know as well. The ring on his finger is usually given after a hunter has proved themselves, after they have displayed their capabilities. But he has it on now, so soon. It's... troubling."

"And that's why we have to be 'going.'" I quoted his mom, and he nodded in agreement. "We're leaving DeBruin?"

"Yes. We must get away from the Fallere circle while we can. Ezra will not stop until he either has your magic or is defeated."

"Define defeated."

He didn't. He sat still, my hand still in his. After a moment, he spoke, but didn't answer my question. "You trusted me, Cecilia. Even after taking your memories, causing you pain, not answering your questions. You still trusted me enough to figure out who I was and go through the gates. Thank you."

"Well, it was either that or have my best friend pin me down and take my magic, probably killing me in the process. Easy choice..."

But Xavier shook his head. "No, it wasn't an easy choice. You had no reason to trust me."

"My gut told me to. My... my heart told me to."

Xavier lifted my hand in his and placed it on his chest. "Mine too, Cecilia. Mine too. You were not what I was expecting when I first met you. Mother wasn't happy with the way I had treated you at first. For that, I apologize."

He shifted and leaned against the wall next to me, our shoulders touching, our hands still clasped. I wasn't sure if it was him or me that didn't want to let go. Maybe both.

"So... you're my protector. Like a bodyguard?" I asked, my eyes still closed. Even though I hadn't done anything, my body was exhausted.

Xavier chuckled. "Sort of. Once you learn to control your magic, you'll be more than capable of protecting yourself."

That reminded me of something. "When Ezra was about to… attack," I said for lack of a better word, "my hands tingled. Like violently. Like they wanted me to *do* something."

"Hmm," Xavier hummed. I opened my eyes slowly and looked over at him. He had turned his head, looking at me, our faces only a few inches away from each other. "That's good. A little concerning, but good."

"Why concerning?" Panic rose in my chest. Xavier obviously knew so much more than I did, and I didn't know what was bad and what was not. From now on, I vowed to myself, I would question *everything*, and not stop until I had concrete answers.

He gave my hand a squeeze before replying. "You're a Chevalier, Cecilia. Descended from one of the original magical families. One of the circles that helped save my kind. Your ancestors were some of the most powerful witches out there. Until…"

My heart fell. "Until Ezra's circle. Until my ancestors declared war on them, getting themselves all killed in the process."

"Aha." Xavier sat up, turning around to face me. "That is where you're wrong, Cecilia. They aren't all dead. Just because a circle looks like it's wiped out doesn't make it so."

I frowned, but then remembered something Ezra had told me he saw in his research. "The research says my line ended with my mother. Yet, here I am, in the flesh." I gestured to myself, as if Xavier didn't realize I was a living human being.

He nodded slowly, his eyes trained on mine. "Exactly. You were left off the line, as no one knew about you, except the Fallere's. They took your grandmother on the off chance your mother was alive. No one expected you to gain your magic without guides."

"How does that make sense?"

"If your mother had died, then the line would sufficiently be cut off. Your powers wouldn't have been strong enough to call *us* here. I believe it was either the moment Ezra's touch burned you, or he saw that," Xavier gestured to the necklace, "on your neck that they realized there was a problem."

"I'm not a problem," I countered immediately.

Xavier grinned, his sparkling white teeth and elongated canines shining in the light coming from torches lining the room. "You most definitely are not a problem, Cecilia Chevalier. Not to me."

CHAPTER 3

T he rumble from my stomach woke me up. After Xavier and I had talked a bit more, my eyelids took over and closed without me even knowing. He had laid me down and found a blanket to cover me.

I rubbed at my eyes before realizing I had put mascara on before school today. Or was it yesterday? It was hard to determine time here in this chamber. How long would I have to stay here? Would I be able to leave, or was Ezra and his family still too big of a risk?

"Hey." A soft voice came from down by my feet.

I stretched my hands over my head, listening to the satisfying cracks from my shoulders and down my back. "Hi. What time is it?"

"About three in the morning. You were out for a good six hours."

"Three in the *morning*?" Oh no, oh no, oh no. I had to get home. Gramps would be beside himself and—

"My mother went to your house. She spoke to your grandfather. Actually, I think she's still there..." Sadness washed over Xavier's features, and I caught on to his meaning immediately.

Elodie was Mom's protector. The vampire who had been keeping her hidden, away from hunters, away from the Fallere circle for eighteen years.

She had been the only one who had seen Mom all this time. Now, she was able to tell Gramps that not only was Mom alive, but she was well. Xavier had told me as such. Only his mother knew Mom's precise whereabouts, as it was too risky otherwise.

Gramps had to be beside himself. After years of making up stories to placate me, and probably his mind as well, he was finally learning the truth.

And if he reacted the same way I had earlier... Then he needed me. I had to be there for him.

I sat up, pushing the blanket away and rolled off the long pillow cushion to get to my feet. The second I did, my head spun.

Xavier flashed in front of me, grabbing my arms and steadying me.

"That's going to take some getting used to," I muttered.

"The dizziness? No, that'll take some food and water to cure," Xavier said.

I shook my head, which was a bad idea. It was a good thing Xavier was strong and could support me until I took a step back and rested against the wall. "No. Your... super speed."

"Ah, yes. It comes in handy, however. Watch this." I didn't even have a chance to turn my head and watch him leave the room before he was back, a cheeseburger and fries in his hand. "One moment," he said as he flashed out of the room. A second later, he returned with a large soda and a bottle of water.

"You ran all the way downtown to get food and back in less time than it took me to breathe?" I held the burger and fries in my hands while Xavier rested the drinks on the floor. I slid down the wall, sitting cross-legged in front of the water bottle.

Xavier joined me. "No. They were in the next room. I grabbed some food while you were asleep. What kind of place would be open at three in the morning anyway?"

I stared at him for a beat, a slow, sly grin creeping up on his face. He wasn't the kind of guy to smile often, but it was becoming more of a thing lately.

And I didn't mind it one bit.

"So what now?" I asked between bites of burger and shoving fries in my face. "Your mom is at my house. Ezra is on the loose. We both obviously ditched school."

"You spelled the nurse to excuse you from school," Xavier interrupted with a knowing look on his face.

"Ugh," I replied. "Can you, like, not be everywhere, all the time, watching and lurking in the shadows?" I was teasing, but it was kind of true.

Xavier lifted a finger. "That's your downfall. I wasn't even lurking. I was standing right outside the nurse's office. Literally followed you the entire way until we got here. I was right behind you the whole time."

My breath caught in my throat. He was there? The whole time? But usually when he was around, that random shiver spread down my spine. I hadn't felt—

"Your magic was building. You were stressed. Overwhelmed. Ignoring all the signs, like you learned to ignore the... what did you call it? The tingle?"

"Your necklace stopped the tingles," I shot back, pointing to it still resting on my chest. "Once I put it on, they stopped."

But he shook his head, disagreeing with me. "It didn't. The necklace knew it found its intended recipient, and the powers went to work. The tingle is still there. You said it yourself. You felt it outside, with Ezra. It's still inside of you, Cecilia."

"The hum." I remembered how the tingle had changed into a low, indistinct hum throughout my body, always there, but deep enough where I didn't focus on it quite like the tingle. "What do you mean, intended recipient?"

Xavier lifted his eyes to meet mine, his dark ones full of mystery. "The necklace was made for you, Cecilia. And only you."

"By who?"

"Me."

I almost dropped the burger that was halfway to my mouth at that point. "You? You made this?"

He nodded slowly, but didn't offer any more. I wanted to dig deep, to ask what the symbol meant, but I didn't have the energy.

"Well, it's beautiful and helpful, so great job. But back to my original question—what now?"

Xavier tucked his lips in, like there was something he wanted to say, but wasn't sure if he should.

"Nope," I said, pointing a fry at him. "That's exactly what we're *not* going to do anymore. I can't handle the secrets. I can't handle the vague, the runaround, the 'don't tell CC because she can't handle it' type of nonsense. If you want to say it, say it."

"There's a lot," he started with a sigh. "We have to get you out of DeBruin safely, to start. Then, we need to find you a guide."

"You mean…" I didn't want to say it. I couldn't get my hopes up.

But Xavier shook his head. "No. Not your mother. Not right away, at least. Putting the two of you in the same place would be like a giant arrow for hunters. And not just for the Fallere circle either."

My eyes practically bugged out of my head. "You mean there are more circles that want me dead? Is there a list or something I can use to keep track of everyone who wants me—" I slid my thumb across my throat with a creaking noise.

"No, Cecilia," Xavier answered, sounding exasperated. Alright, maybe now wasn't the time to make jokes. Got it.

"Sorry," I whispered, sensing his disappointment in me. Once again, I said the wrong thing at the wrong time.

"Cecilia," Xavier said, shuffling across the cold, hard ground to be closer to me. He moved the food and drinks out of the way, coming as close to me as possible. Then, he lifted my chin, staring directly into my eyes when he said, "I cannot talk about you dying. Please. If there ever was a nightmare for me, it is that. I have sworn my life to protect you, and nothing will get me to break it."

"Why, though? What if you wanted to go off and live your own life, to not be chained to me for the rest of mine? What happens if I do die? I'm sorry, I know you said you can't talk about it, but I need to know everything, Xavier."

His grip on my chin tightened as his name rolled off my lips, but he didn't look away. Instead, he got closer, almost close enough for me... for me to kiss him.

My breath hitched, and my heart raced. If I was *anywhere* else, with *anyone* else, in *any* other circumstance, I would take the chance. I would lean forward just an inch and place my lips on his.

Like Ezra had just the other night.

"Cecilia Chevalier, my life has been yours since the day you were born."

Somehow his accent had gotten thicker in the past moment, and it made my insides flip flop.

"That is how it is with witches and their vampire protectors. We give our lives for you. If you die... I die."

CHAPTER 4

Kissing Xavier was erased from my mind the moment he let that bomb drop.

"Excuse me? Did I just hear you right?" I scrambled out of his grasp and to my feet, suddenly not hungry anymore. "You just said that if I die, you die. Like, automatically? That's the price you pay for losing me? Your *life*?"

Xavier stood as well, towering over me by almost a foot, but his stance wasn't intimidating. I half expected him to drop to his knees and pledge his loyalty or something. "Yes, Cecilia. That is how it works. That is how it has worked for centuries between witches and our vampires."

"He's right," a female voice floated in from behind me. I spun around, finding Elodie in the doorway. "It is the vow we take, but do not think for one moment, sweet Cecilia, that we regret it. Not ever. The witches gave us our lives, and we repay them with ours, if we fail to do our job."

"It just seems a little... extreme, is all I'm saying."

Elodie tilted her head, her long, dark hair falling into her face, a small smile crossing her lips. She and Xavier looked so much alike it was almost unsettling. Though the looks Xavier usually gave me were more emotional, more fierce, more... strict. It was slightly refreshing to see a comforting look for once.

"It is our way. Now, child, we must be going." She turned to leave, probably expecting us to just blindly follow her, like

Xavier was already doing. He made it two feet before he looked back over his shoulder to see that I hadn't moved.

"Wait. Go where? What about Gramps?" Say his name made a sob catch in my throat. Would I ever be able to see him again? Was he going to be safe here?

Elodie stopped just past the doorway, looking first at her son, then at me. "That is exactly where I am taking you, sweet Cecilia. Times may be dire, but family always comes first."

I let out a sigh of relief, my shoulders sagging. This was all just so much, neither my mind nor my body could comprehend.

Xavier stepped back and placed his hands on my shoulders. "Cecilia."

"Xavier."

Something in my chest burst at that moment, the necklace growing warm, my heart constricting and expanding at the same time. His grip on me tightened, but I could see the slight grimace on his face.

"We won't let anything happen to you. To your grandfather. To your mother. This I swear upon. But you need to know how strong *you* are, Cecilia. How much I believe in you. How powerful you will become. But it is all a testament to you. Your strength. Your bravery. Tell me, Cecilia, when Ezra attacked, what was your first instinct?"

I couldn't look away from him. It was like he had a hold on me, on my attention, on my body, on my heart. "I wanted to fight. I wanted to protect myself. I wanted to protect you. My hands tingled, wanting to just snap away until everything was done."

"And then I told you to go through the gates. You listened without hesitation. You trusted me—"

"I trusted you because my gut told me it was the right thing to do."

"How many times have you listened to that instinct, and it turned out to be correct?" The smirk on his face got me now.

"Funny. Sure, my weakness is not thinking things through a lot. But... whatever you say, Xavier, I'll do. No matter what."

"You will only get stronger, Cecilia. Things will change from here, but we have no doubt you'll adapt. You'll grow. You'll do amazing things."

His words filled me with a confidence I never knew existed. The warmth of the necklace spread through me, pushing away the tingles, silencing the hum, charging me with something new I couldn't place.

"We must go," Elodie said softly. I nodded, suddenly no longer afraid of leaving the chamber. Xavier slid his hands down my arms and intertwined his fingers with mine.

"We're going to do this together. I will not leave your side, Cecilia."

"I mean, if I die, you die. No pressure there, right?" Now it seemed like an okay time to joke. We had our serious talks all night. We were about to embark on an adventure I wasn't sure I could handle, but knew he would help me through no matter what.

"None at all."

As we exited the chamber and stood in the cemetery, it struck me just how *quiet* it was. It wasn't a scary quiet, but more of a peaceful, soothing silence.

"Now we go home? What if Ezra is out?"

Xavier smiled at me. "He's still the same inexperienced hunter he was a few hours ago. That hasn't changed. He is no match for me."

I wanted to roll my eyes at his macho-man energy, but I refrained.

"Besides, we're more worried about his mother and whatever other circle members live in this town," Elodie added.

That chilled me to my bones. This whole time there had been witches living in DeBruin and I had no idea. Not even once I discovered my magic. They were *right here*, yet they weren't here to help me. They were here to harm me.

"What if we come across some of them?" I breathed, following Elodie as we made our way toward the gates.

"You have your protection on. Xavier is trained. And you have your magic, don't forget. Feel like getting a little nervous tension out?" Elodie grinned.

"Wha—wha—what?" I stumbled over a tree root in the dark, but Xavier caught me. "You want me to use it? Won't that, like, give me away?"

"Not within the cemetery it won't. That's why you had to come through here while I took care of Ezra. It's spelled to protect against outside forces. In here, they cannot sense you. They cannot find your magic." Xavier said it like he himself had put the protection over the area. Maybe he had. He seemed to be able to do things that were magic-like, even without being a witch. Or a warlock. A wizard? I had yet to get clarification on technicalities.

I let go of his hand and flexed my fingers, stretching them out, then shaking my arms loose. I hadn't snapped since leaving the nurse yesterday, and not much before then. Ezra had scared it out of me.

"What should I do?" I had nothing in my mind to focus on; everything else was taking up so much space, I was scared I would blow up half the cemetery at that point.

"Just snap, darling. See what happens." Elodie sounded confident, but it did not translate to me.

"That... usually ends badly," I admitted, my cheeks flushing.

"*That* was before you learned who you are. Who your family is. That was before your protection wards. That was then. This is now. Go for it."

I had no idea what she meant. All I heard was 'go for it.' And that was all I needed.

Snap snap.

A second later, I was hovering in the air, Xavier reaching up to grab me, but I lifted higher and higher. Elodie's lithe laughter followed me as I flipped onto my back, laying as if in a bed.

"Cecilia!" cried Xavier, slight terror in his voice. He was concerned, obviously, but there was nothing to worry about.

I had never felt safer.

"Now *this* is what I'm talking about! Who needs a broom when I can just—oh no!" Maybe my magic wasn't as powerful as I thought, or maybe I needed a bit more practice, but my sudden flying session came to an abrupt end a second later, sending me plummeting a good ten feet to the ground.

Or... right into Xavier's arms. He flashed from where he had been standing, positioning himself directly under me, his arms outstretched. I landed in them gently, barely moving his stoic body.

Grinning, I looked up at him, only to find him with a frown and furrowed brows. "Come on, Xavier. Live a little! You have to admit, that was freaking amazing!"

He just shook his head, lifting me slightly, almost as if he were pulling me into his chest like a hug. "Don't do that again, Cecilia. Please."

A second later, he put me down on my feet, where I brushed off my hands and looked at Elodie. "What else can I do?"

Her head cocked as she looked at her son, who still looked like he wanted to vomit. Then, she turned to me. "Your magic is a part of you. Whatever is deepest in your soul will manifest, if you do not focus on something specific."

I shrugged. "Makes sense. I've always wanted to fly. Maybe I'll get myself a broom."

"We must be going. Plenty of time for you to keep practicing later." Elodie headed toward the gates, Xavier and I following her.

Xavier slid next to me, walking shoulder to shoulder. Part of me wanted him to reach for my hand again, but I didn't quite know how to ask. And I wasn't brave enough just yet to do it myself.

"Just so you know," Xavier said, leaning in closer to me to whisper in my ear, "witches don't ride brooms."

"Just so you know," I responded, "that's quite the disappointment."

CHAPTER 5

"Don't ring the doorbell," I muttered just loud enough for Elodie to hear. She didn't ask why, but knocked lightly instead. Having just come from here, I had no doubt Gramps was still awake despite the ridiculously late hour.

"Gramps!" I exclaimed the moment he opened the front door. I went to launch myself at him, never having been happier to see the man in my life.

"Inside, child, inside." Elodie looked around side to side, her lips in a thin line. Xavier had taken up residence behind her, his back to us as he scanned the street.

"Please, Elodie, Xavier, come in, come in." Gramps ushered us all inside, closing the door and locking it behind us. Then, finally, he turned and wrapped his arms around me. "My dear CC, I am so sorry for everything that has happened. I should have prepared you. I should have told you. I should—"

"Stop it, you old grump. If everything that these two have told me is true, then you've been the only reason I've made it this far in life. And truthfully, I haven't made that easy on you, have I?" I couldn't help the giggle that escaped. Even Xavier took a moment from staring through the window to look over his shoulder and roll his eyes at me.

"You are spectacular, Cecilia. Exactly like your mother in every way. If only your grandmother was here, she could have taught you, guided you..."

I hugged him again. "You've done a spectacular job. Now it's up to me to figure things out. Think of it as me going away to college. Although, I have no idea where we're *actually* going, but still."

Gramps let go of me and hurried into the living room. There, he threw the rug back, exposing a door in the wooden floorboards.

"Um, *excuse me*, where did that come from and why have I never known it was there?" I put my hands on my hips and pouted. "That would have made an amazing junk food stash."

Gramps let out a signature 'hrumph' and continued moving boards and reaching down. Whatever was under there must have been heavy, because he was struggling.

Xavier tore his attention away from the window long enough to notice and headed over toward Gramps.

"Wait. I think I can handle this," I said, putting an arm out to stop him. When my arm connected with him, that deep-rooted shiver came back.

But I didn't have time to dissect what that meant. I had witchiness to do.

Snap snap.

Gramps fell back on his bottom as a large chest rose from under the floor, over the couch, and almost crashed into Elodie before she ducked.

"Umm..." I wrung my hands together, unsure on how to stop the chest from floating around the entire house, knocking over pictures on the wall and vases on tables.

"Cecilia." Xavier took my attention back. One look at him calmed my mind.

Snap snap.

I completely expected the chest to slam into the ground the same way I almost did as I hovered, but it didn't. It slowly lowered itself at the bottom of the stairs, just out of sight of the windows next to the front door. Once it landed, the top popped open with a soft click, releasing a cloud of dust in its wake.

"Cecilia," Gramps said in his warning tone. I looked over at him, his gray brows pulled together so tightly they almost made one unibrow. "That was unnecessary and—"

"She's practicing, Victor," Elodie said softly, placing a hand on Gramp's shoulder and offering her other to help him rise. "She's already doing much better since her protection ward activated."

There she went again talking about something I wasn't too sure of, in a moment I didn't have time to question it. Wherever we were headed, I hoped it was a *long* flight, and I would have nothing to do besides grill her for information.

"Um, Gramps? The chest? Are we going to just stare at it like some magnificent piece of art or are we digging in?" I mimed using a shovel, but he didn't even crack a smile. Which, in turn, made me burst out laughing. It was hard to make him break, and every time I tried and failed only brought me more happiness. Deep down, I knew he was with me.

He shuffled his way over, passing Xavier with narrowed eyes like it was the first time he realized Xavier was in his house. Or maybe he was connecting the dots to the guy who made him sneak my headphones and necklace upstairs while I slept.

"This chest is everything your mother and grandmother had from their circle. Family trees. All sorts of trinkets and doo-dads," Gramps said, taking a moment to kneel in front of it all.

Elodie's face went pale. Well, paler than it already was. "Celeste has been searching for this for years," she whispered, reaching out to touch the edge of the lid. "She thought it was all lost."

Gramp's shoulders sagged at the mention of Mom's name. "I kept everything I had. Everything she sent. Everything Collette could find over the years. When Celeste left, all we had was Cecilia and this small box." He leaned into the chest and pulled out something no bigger than a shoebox. He handed it straight to me.

But I couldn't bring myself to open it right away. I held it for a moment, the weight surprising me. All these years, I assumed

Mom dropped me off with her parents and fled, never looking back, never thinking about me again.

This box proved otherwise. This whole chest proved otherwise. Everything Elodie had said about her made it seem like Mom *never* stopped thinking about me. That the reason she left was to protect me.

"Cecilia," Xavier whispered, his breath tickling my ear as he stood right behind me. Hearing him say my name gave me the confidence and motivation I needed to go forward. I never wanted to stop hearing him say it.

Shifting the box to one hand, I quickly took the lid off, peering inside as soon as I did. There were four items in it, each carefully laid out, looking untouched.

"I never opened it. Collette put it in the chest as soon as we brought you inside. She probably knew what was inside, and I never questioned it," Gramps said, his voice still a bit hoarse.

Elodie took the lid from me, then held the box out so I could lift the items inside. First, a small, blue velvet covered jewelry box. Inside was a ring.

It was gorgeous. A delicate silver band, nothing ornate, nothing outrageous. Four prongs held up a red gemstone, one I couldn't name off the top of my head. Around the stone was a row of silver swirls, just big enough to encircle the round cut stone and showcase the incredible detail.

Just like the necklace, that was it. Simple, but beautiful.

"Oh, Cecilia," Elodie gasped. She stared from the ring to me and back. "You must put it on immediately."

I didn't hesitate, and slid it over my right index finger, somehow knowing that it would fit perfectly. The moment I did, my hand filled with warmth, like a ray of sunshine filling me from within, spreading through my arm and all the way around my body. Then, what felt like sparkles followed. My eyes grew wide as I watched, a glow starting from my finger and traveling up my arm, eventually filling my entire body like the warmth, before casting a bright light that pulsed from my skin and burst outward, leaving little sparkles in its wake.

Xavier, Elodie, and Gramps shielded their eyes from the brightness for a moment, before staring back at me. Elodie had a gentle smile on her face, Gramps looked utterly terrified, and Xavier... Xavier's eyes looked at me, full of wonder and... something else I couldn't quite place. In a heartbeat, he returned to the front, keeping watch from the window.

"I don't think you'll have an issue with your magic anymore," Elodie said, her voice full of awe. "That ring belongs to your circle, traditionally given to young witches when they develop their magic. Your mother couldn't remember if she had put it in the box, or if you had even gotten the box. She'll be glad to hear it is with its rightful owner now."

Feeling strong, confident, and like I could take on the world right now, I looked back into the box and pulled out a book. It was small, with a brown leather cover and a long string winding around it.

"The spell book," Elodie whispered. "She really prepared you in the best way she knew how. Oh, what the Fallere's would give to have that book..." She sighed. "They've been searching for centuries for this book, ever since Sonya left it behind..."

"S—S—Sonya? The one who married into Ezra's family?" I muttered, finally connecting some dots here.

"The one and the same."

This was Sonya's spell book. The girl my family deemed kidnapped. Which side was right? If she married, why wouldn't she have kept her spell book? According to Ezra, she was one of the most powerful witches of the time. Wouldn't she have needed her spell book?

If so... did that mean she *was* kidnapped?

I shook my head and put the book back in the box and looked over at the last two things inside. An envelope, with my name on it, and a picture.

I grabbed the photo first, lifting it out carefully by the edges.

"That's... that's Mom," I whispered. If it wasn't for the clothing, I would have almost said it was *me*.

But as soon as I brought it closer to my face, it changed. Right before my eyes, the picture *changed*. Now, another auburn-haired girl stood next to a tall, wrought-iron fence, a soft smile on her face.

"Your grandmother," Elodie said softly.

I barely had a moment to look before it flipped again. Five more times it shuffled through, all the women with the same hair and eyes as mine, looking almost like we were—

"Your family, Cecilia. Your circle. Going all the way back to Seraphine. Sonya's sister."

This was too much. Too much at once. Here I was holding a magical photo of all the witch women in my family for centuries, while wearing a ring that held some sort of key to my magic, a necklace that protected me against hunters and was connected to Xavier. How, I wasn't sure, but deep down I knew it was. I stood in the entryway to my childhood home, next to two vampires sworn to protect me, learning about my mother who fled to protect me, and in front of a spell book for a formidable witch that had been kidnapped, which started a war between circles.

That ended with *my* circle basically eliminated.

I took in a deep breath, trying to settle my nerves, trying to compartmentalize all of these new things, but I couldn't.

Not until an icy hand laid on my arm. It was only then that my mind cleared, pushing away everything that didn't need to be worried about right now. My necklace warmed, my ring pulsed, and suddenly, it was like I could see clearly.

I put the picture back in the box and reached for the envelope. The teal ink with my name on the outside had faded slightly over time, but I just knew it was Mom's handwriting.

Right as I turned it over to open it, Xavier's grip on my arm tightened.

"We need to go. Now."

CHAPTER 6

E lodie flashed over to the door, leaving me standing with the envelope dangling in my hands. She peered out of the window, her chin lifting, her jaw tightening. "Yes. We must go."

"What's happening?" Gramps asked. He steadied one hand on the edge of the chest and the other on the stair banister, trying to get himself to his feet.

Before I could reach out to him to help, Xavier flashed over, lifting him to his feet effortlessly.

"Outside. They know we're here."

I paled. "Who's outside? It's not even sunrise yet."

He didn't have to answer the question.

Ezra.

And by the worried look on Elodie's face, potentially his family as well. How many of them, I wasn't sure.

"What do we do? How do we get out? What about Gramps?" I shot question after question at Elodie, panicking only slightly.

It was odd. Usually, I would usually be a jumbled mess with all this uncertainty. But right now, I felt almost empowered. Like I wanted to make the decisions and get everyone to safety on my own. I wanted to fight. I wanted to do my part in protecting my family, protecting myself, protecting Xavier and Elodie.

My necklace warmed and my new ring glowed on my hand.

Before I knew what I was doing I snapped.

Snap snap.

"Cecilia!" Xavier exclaimed, but froze in place a second later. "What did you do?"

Elodie glanced between me and the window, her brows raising, her lips parting ever so slightly at whatever she was seeing outside. "They're... turning around. Not leaving, but looking on the other side of the street."

An overwhelming amount of pride flowed through me. "I switched the houses."

"You did *what*?" everyone around me cried at the same time.

Lifting my hand, I inspected my nails, trying to be modest and humble, but it was no use. I was *flipping out* inside and I couldn't contain it. "I switched the houses! At least, an image of them. We're still here, obviously," I waved around, showing them that nothing had changed. "But to them, the image they see is that our house is the one across the street. This one looks like that one. Just on the outside though. That's why they turned around. They thought they were watching the wrong house."

Xavier's whole face went stoic for a moment before he lifted the corner of his mouth in a slight grin. It wasn't the broad beaming smile I had seen earlier, but it was enough. "You're a genius, Cecilia Chevalier. And... *powerful*. That is magic I haven't seen anyone your age ever do. A cloaking spell..."

"She is the daughter of Celeste, a descendent of the Potentia family. It is not unheard of. Unexpected, but not unheard of. But now we must go. Through the back." Elodie let the curtain drop and headed toward the kitchen.

But I stayed put. "What about Gramps?"

Xavier reached me first, his hands on my shoulders again. "They don't want him. They won't hurt him, unless they suspect he is hiding you. Which is why it's best that we leave, immediately. You are strong, much stronger than we, or they, know. They will do everything they can to get to you, and right now there are more of them than us. Even as vampires, we have our limitations against witches, especially when a circle of three or more have convened."

"Do they have vampires helping them too?"

Xavier's eyes softened. "Some. That's another story for another time. Now, say your goodbyes. You won't be coming back for a while."

He turned to join his mother in the kitchen while I looked over at Gramps. He had tears in his eyes, which made mine well up immediately.

"Gramps..."

Instead of talking, he reached forward and wrapped me in the tightest hug I ever had from him. I wound my arms around his torso, burying my face into his shoulder.

"You are just like your mother. Your grandmother. You can do this, Cecilia. I am so sorry I didn't adequately prepare you for this new life of yours, but I know you'll be able to handle it."

I sniffled, then nodded. "I'll do my best."

"You'll make me proud. You always do."

"Cecilia!" Elodie called.

Gramps held me out at arms-length, taking one last look at me. I did the same to him. Then, he hugged me once more and ushered me to the hallway.

"Cecilia?" he called out just before we made it to the back door. I glanced over my shoulder at him, finding tears openly streaming down his cheeks now. "When you find your mother... Please tell her I love her." He waved a hand as Elodie ushered me out of the house, the box tucked under her arm, and closed the door behind me.

We stood in the backyard, me with the unopened envelope in my hand, her with the box, and Xavier reaching for my hand. He clasped it tightly, pulling me closer to him.

"Um, now what? I cloaked the front of the house, but I don't know how long it'll hold. I'm guessing just walking out of here won't be the easy plan..."

Elodie looked at me, glancing down at Xavier and I holding hands. I hadn't thought much of it, not until a look crossed her face. "Now, we need *you*, Cecilia. When you first called to us, we were transported here immediately. You are the one who can take us where we need to go."

"Which is...?" It suddenly occurred to me that I had no idea where Xavier and Elodie had been before coming to DeBruin. Wherever it was, was where my mother was as well. But they said I couldn't go to her, not yet.

Elodie shrugged. "Anywhere but this town. Outside city limits, it'll take more effort for them to find us. It doesn't have to be far, as we don't want to overextend your magic too soon, but somewhere other than here."

"Oh. Right." So no snapping our way to Italy, I supposed. "Well then—wait. What if this doesn't work? What if I can't get all three of us there?"

"Then I stay with you, no matter what," Xavier replied instantly, squeezing my hand.

Elodie nodded. "The two of you absolutely cannot be separated."

"You're going to get so sick of me," I joked, giving Xavier a side eye with a smirk. He shook his head, but I could tell he was biting back a smile. Turning to Elodie, I asked, "Can you put this back in the box? I'll have to open it later. I trust you to keep it all safe."

"If we get separated, I will return to your mother and deliver this. We will wait for you. Xavier will know how to find me when the time is right."

"You say that like you expect—"

A dart of red light streaked by me just then, narrowly avoiding hitting my shoulder. I shrieked and turned toward Xavier, who threw an arm around me and crouched to the ground.

Elodie ripped the envelope out of my hands, stuffed it into the box, and exclaimed, "Go! You must go now! I'll fend them off while you escape!"

My hands shook, but the warmth from the necklace and the power from the ring returned. Xavier gently placed his hand on my chin, lifting it to look me in the eye. No words exchanged between us as he moved his head in the smallest of nods, never breaking eye contact.

Snap snap.

CHAPTER 7

"Cecilia?" Worry laced Xavier's voice. "Cecilia!" His hand was still intertwined with mine, but my arm was outstretched, bent at an odd angle. I felt him let go, and all of the sudden, I was tumbling through time and space, unable to catch on to anything to steady myself.

I flew through the air, twirling, circling head over heels again and again until—

I stopped. My head spun, but my body slammed into the ground with a force that would rival an Air Force pilots.

Or so it seemed. Once everything was back in its rightful spot, I opened my eyes, finding myself standing, wrapped in Xavier's arms, one around my shoulders and the other around my waist, pulling me flush into him. He tucked my head on his shoulder and was whispering something I couldn't make out.

"What... What happened? Where are we?" I muttered.

Xavier froze, but it didn't last long. Slowly he pulled away, separating us by only a few inches.

"You're okay?" His voice was gravelly, like he was forcing the words out.

"Kind of feel like I've been put through a blender, but otherwise, yes. You?"

He nodded, his lips pressed together.

"Your mom. Oh my gosh, Xavier, your mom. We left her behind!"

But he didn't even blink. He hadn't moved, his eyes glued to mine. "You're okay. Cecilia, I..."

The way he was looking at me sent one of those deep shivers down my spine. The ones I only had when around him. I used to hate it, knowing that it meant he was there, watching, lurking, listening.

Now, though... Now I craved it in the same way I craved him saying my name. The way he said it made my insides flip flop, my heart race, while also calming me in a way only he could.

"Xavier..."

"Cecilia..."

The softness in his eyes spread, the tightness in his jaw loosening, his shoulders dropping. My chest was still pressed to his, one of his hands on my hip, holding me in place, the other having moved to the back of my neck.

A split second later, the entire world around me exploded.

Xavier leaned down, gently placing his lips on mine, as if waiting for a full invitation. I responded by lifting onto my tiptoes slightly, getting closer to him while kissing him back.

He tensed for a moment before winding his icy fingers up into my hair, pressing into me with such force that I felt like maybe we really were flying.

I didn't open my eyes to check, though, not caring if we were. Because right now, my chest was on fire, my hands burning, my entire body feeling like a million stars had burst inside of me and any second I would scatter back to the earth in a shower of sparkles.

This kiss... this one flipped my world upside down in the best possible way. This one felt as if I had been living with only half my heart, but now it was whole.

I never wanted this kiss to end.

But Xavier being Xavier broke apart a few minutes later, his chest heaving, his grip still holding me down. We were not, in fact, flying. We were rooted to the ground, standing chest to chest, as he rested his forehead on mine.

"Cecilia…"

"Say it again."

"Cecilia Potentia Chevalier." He stated it so confidently, so matter-of-factly, like he had been saying it his whole life.

It was only then that a terrible pain erupted on my chest, the necklace singeing through my shirt, a blistering heat attacking the skin beneath it.

At the same moment, Xavier let me go, doubling over with his own hands clutching at his chest. I dropped to my knees, the pain overwhelming, searing.

Just when my vision began to go black, when there was no air left in my lungs, when it felt like I couldn't handle any more…

It stopped.

I gasped, desperate for oxygen, needing to breathe to make sure I was safe. That I was alive.

"What… was… that?" I huffed, casting a glance toward Xavier, who had fallen on one knee, an elbow resting on it, his head hung. For the first time, I saw him with his hair messy, hanging down over his face like he had been tugging at the strands.

He looked… ridiculously hot. Hotter than I had thought he had been before, accent and all.

"Cecilia?" His head shot up, his eyes meeting mine in an instant. "You… you felt that?"

I gestured to my necklace, looping my pinky through the chain so I didn't have to touch what I assumed was hot metal. "This? Yeah. It burned right through my…" I stopped, realizing my clothes had no trace of a burn on them. Then how did I feel it branding my skin beneath?

Xavier stood, stretching his arms behind him and taking off his black long-sleeved shirt in a quick swoop. I openly gawked, knowing he had been hiding a decent physique under the layers, but not expecting what I saw.

His fair skin highlighted every ab, the definition of his pecs, the V muscles from his hips. But that wasn't what I focused on.

The bright red, newly branded, burned skin right under his collarbone in the middle of his chest was.

It was in the same pattern as the necklace I wore around my neck. The one he had taken off of himself and given to me, as protection from hunters.

The symbol I couldn't figure out until I saw it clearly now, on him.

It wasn't snakes. It wasn't random squiggles.

It was an X and a C intertwined, with flourishes.

"What...?" I mumbled, unsure where to even begin. The necklace burned me because it rested on my body. How did the same design end up on him, causing him the same pain?

Xavier crossed the few steps over to me, grabbed my hands and lifted me to my feet. Then, he gently pushed the collar of my sweater down until he found what he was looking for.

The same symbol, in the same place.

"This... this hasn't happened in centuries," Xavier mumbled. "So long that I thought it wasn't even true."

"Thought *what* wasn't true? What is this? Why did it burn me? I thought the protection was against hunters, that it made a hunter's touch burn. How did you—"

"I made the charm, Cecilia. I had the protection put on it. But... this," he gestured to his mark then mine, "can't be what I think it is. Not even my mother has seen it."

"Xavier," I pleaded, getting his attention enough to look at me. "Please, just tell me."

He let my shirt go, but didn't move his hand away from my shoulder. "There have been stories passed down throughout generations about fate."

"Fate?"

He nodded. "Centuries ago, after the witches saved the vampires, there had been pairings that fell in love. Not many, but a few. Both sides were against it, knowing that it would never work. But each time, there were marks that appeared on each other, symbolizing what we called fate. A mark of fate meant both sides were to leave the couple alone, that there was a bigger calling for them as a pair."

I blinked. Then blinked again because *what*? Xavier and I were... fated? Meant to be together?

"I have been sworn to be your protector since the moment I was born, Cecilia," Xavier stated.

"Which was... how long ago exactly?" I never thought to ask that before now, even though I knew in stories vampires could be hundreds of years old. The thought creeped me out—I really didn't want to be going around kissing a five-hundred-year-old man...

"Twenty years and six months ago," Xavier said, a lopsided grin on his face. "Remember, fiction and reality are different. Mother was your mother's protector long before I came, and when I did, I was bound to be yours."

"Whew. Okay, that's great. Because... yeah. Anyway. You were sworn to be my protector even though you didn't know I would even develop my magic?"

He nodded. "If you hadn't, we probably would never have met. But you did, and here we are. The fates never lie, Cecilia. Witches depend on it."

"So we got burned and branded because what, we kissed?"

For that, he only shrugged. "I do not know how it works. Like I said, I never thought it was real."

"You said centuries ago... When was the last fated pair?"

Xavier became very quiet then, his hands dropping completely from my body, hanging at his sides limply. He stared off into the distance, his eyes glazed over slightly, like he was dissociating from himself.

"Xavier?"

Immediately, his attention snapped to mine. "Apologies. I was trying to remember. My mother used to tell me stories as a child, of fated loves, of how witches saved the vampires, of our vow to continue to save them from hunters. It's all intertwined, but those stories specifically..."

He trailed off, thinking again. "I can only remember one. But I cannot remember any names associated with it."

I reached out and laid my hand on his arm. "What do you remember?"

Xavier took a deep breath, then shut his eyes briefly before opening them to meet mine. "There was a young, powerful witch. One of the best in her circle, even from a young age. She developed her powers earlier than most, and was strong from the start. She was special. The circle knew they had to protect her the most, as did the vampires. Hunters were after her all the time, from many circles, but none could get close."

I tucked my lips in, biting down to keep myself from interrupting. I already had so many questions, but it wasn't the time.

"As she got older, her magic grew stronger. She was the best of her circle, the best out of many. Her protector stayed by her side night and day, never leaving her alone. Until one day, she compromised—if he could make her a medallion, she would spell it, and it could help protect her from hunters."

I reached up and grabbed my necklace, now cooled off. "Like this?"

Xavier nodded. "It's where I got the idea, I think. Many vampires are skilled metallurgists. Your mother spelled it. My mother brought it to her, and she did it immediately, even though she hadn't used that sort of magic in years. I wore it for three years before you called, hoping to give it to you one day."

Tears prickled at the corner of my eyes. He had already done so much for me, more than I could even imagine, more than I could repay him for.

"Tell me the rest."

"She wore the medallion at all times, even when he was with her. She never took it off. Until one day, a few years later, when she was older, she told him she loved him. He told her the same."

Xavier paused, and I held my breath, waiting to hear what came next.

"I... I can't remember exactly what happened after that, but there was some turmoil between the witches and the vampires. They didn't want them to be together, mixing the vampire's responsibilities with love. But the young witch and the vampire couldn't stop it. One day, not long after, while the witch was with her circle, the medallion began to burn, like yours, and she ripped it off. But she was left with a mark, on her wrist, where she wore her medallion like a bracelet. She was scared, and the witches blamed the vampire."

"She took off the protection?"

Xavier nodded, looking solemn. "The witches kept her from her vampire for a few days, trying to figure out what to do and why they couldn't undo the burn mark."

My heart raced, already understanding where Xavier was going.

"A day later, she was gone. The hunters found her, and without the medallion, she was defenseless except for her magic."

"They drained her."

At this, Xavier shook his head. "No. Worse. They kept her, forcing her to live and stay within their circle. Her circle and the vampires tried to get her back, declaring war on the kidnappers, but—"

I held up a hand. "Wait. War? Kidnapping? Xavier... are you talking about... about *Sonya*?"

CHAPTER 8

"What did you say?" Xavier asked, his eyes darkening.

"Sonya. The girl that got kidnapped by Ezra's family circle. The one he said my circle declared war on his because they took her. But he said his family insists that she married someone from their family and left willingly. I didn't know which one was right, not until Sonya's spell book was in that box my mother left for me. If she was as powerful as everyone says, she wouldn't have just left her spell book behind, would she?"

Xavier looked at me, still confused. "You're saying... the stories about fated love all stem from Sonya, the girl who started the war? The kidnapped Sonya?"

"Yes! Oh, can't you see it now? She had to have been kidnapped! She wouldn't have left her fated vampire like that! Like you said, she was powerful enough where they didn't even want to drain her. They wanted to use her. Remember the picture in the box? How I was related to her sister, Seraphine?"

Xavier nodded, looking down at our hands between us. "Cecilia... that story. If it's not just fiction and it's real, then this... us... we're just like them. You, an incredibly powerful young witch, and me, the... the..."

"The vampire in love with her that vows to protect her with his life?"

He nodded, but didn't look up just yet.

We stood in silence, taking everything from the past few minutes in.

Finding the box. Leaving Gramps. Being attacked. Leaving Elodie. My magic landing us here, wherever it was we were. Kissing Xavier. The necklace. The fates.

"You need to rest," Xavier finally said. For some reason, he looked defeated. I stepped back, unsure what to do next, what to think next.

Was he upset by the whole thing? He kissed me first. Obviously neither of us was expecting all of this, but was there anything we could do?

Or was it because I put his feelings out there, into the world, when he had tried to shut them away?

If I died, he died. That was the rule.

But nowhere in the rule book did it state he had to fall in love with me first.

Or I with him.

"Back to the original question—where are we?" The sun was just over the horizon now, which meant hours had to have passed since we left home. Who knew how long we were knocked out on the ground for?

Xavier was right, though. I was exhausted. The level of magic it must have taken to get us here was way more than anything I had used before. The ring must have helped, like Elodie said it would, but it still was a lot.

"I'll find out. You..." Xavier glanced around, searching our new surroundings, "stay over here."

For the first time, I looked around with actual interest. We were on the outskirts of a forest of some kind, next to a path that led into the woods. Xavier took my hand and brought me into the trees, settling me down behind a few a little ways in.

"Rest, if you can. I'll find some food and figure out where we are. In the meantime—"

"No funny business. No causing chaos. No snapping," I said before he could get the words out. I sank to the forest floor, crunching some dead leaves in the process. "I know."

Xavier crouched in front of me, resting his elbows on his knees, and reaching out to lift my chin. "Cecilia Chevalier, you do whatever needs to be done to protect yourself. Your instincts will take you far and you are much more capable than anyone has given you an opportunity to prove. Just know, large amounts of magic can be detected."

Once again, his words filled me with the confidence I seemed to continue to lack. He knew exactly when I needed a pep talk too.

"I'll be back soon."

He took off, soundlessly jogging through the forest floor. I frowned, wondering why he didn't just use his crazy super speed, then realized something.

We barely knew each other.

I had no idea how his life as a vampire worked. He knew nothing of me prior to showing up in DeBruin. The only reason we were attached to each other was the circumstances we found ourselves in. Of course, he had a slight advantage, knowing *of* me before meeting me, but that wasn't much to go on.

I leaned back against the tree, closing my eyes. Every part of my body was exhausted but also still a bit exhilarated. My mind was running a mile a minute, worrying, thinking, planning. Where did we go from here? How could we outrun Ezra's family... and Ezra? Did my best friend turned enemy hate me or the idea of me because of what his family said?

The biggest thing I thought of right now was Sonya. What if I could somehow tell Ezra about Sonya and her protector and tell him she really was kidnapped? He would believe me, wouldn't he? Or did his family circle already brainwash him into believing lies?

Eventually, the fatigue took over, and I fell asleep, leaning against the tree, with one hand wrapped around my necklace.

"Cecilia. Cecilia, wake up."

My body went straight into fight-or-flight mode, which, somehow, meant I accessed both parts at once. I leapt to my feet, snapping my fingers without even realizing it, and ended up in a tree fifteen feet off the ground, with Xavier spread out on the forest floor in a daze.

"Oh no, oh no, oh no!" I cried, my hands flying to cover my face in embarrassment. "Oh, what did I do?"

"Remind me... Never wake a sleeping Cecilia..." Xavier huffed, pushing himself onto his elbows and staring up at me. His hair was still rumpled, the white streak mixing in with the rest of the dark, charcoal strands. Some of it hung over his forehead, making him look slightly less serious, but a lot hotter. He had put his shirt back on before leaving, but now it had ridden up his torso slightly, exposing his abs once again.

"I'm sorry! I guess I'm a little bit more on edge than I thought I was." I looked down at my hands, a little worried at how fast they responded and did what they wanted without me even thinking about it. "Um, is this normal by the way? I'm not used to snapping without having to focus super intensely on it."

Xavier reached up and pushed his hair back, frowning, but keeping his eyes on me. "Normally, for brand new witches, no. But... you aren't really the same as any other brand new witches I've seen before, Cecilia. You're different. Stronger. More powerful. Your mind seems more in tune with your magic than most witches, even those many years older than you."

I cringed. The *last* thing I needed was to have *more* magic than normal, especially when I had no idea what to do with it and wasn't allowed to use a lot of it right now.

"Cecilia?" Xavier called. I glanced down finding him sitting up now, his legs bent, his arms resting on his black jeans clad knees. He looked so relaxed, so at ease. Something I hadn't really seen him be yet, except back in the chamber in the cemetery. "Are you coming down?"

"Oh! Right..." I looked around, trying to figure out if any of the other branches would be strong enough to hold me on my descent.

A laugh from down below got my attention. Xavier was now standing at the base of the tree, leaning against it, shaking his head.

"What now?"

"You, Cecilia. Sometimes I forget how new this all is to you."

"Why yes, Xavier, this is my first time being stuck in a tree, thanks for asking. Instead of laughing, could you maybe help me down? What kind of protector are you?"

But he only laughed again as he looked up at me, grinning. "How did you get up there?"

"Well, it was a combination of being scared to death and my body reacting by—Oh." I caught on quickly.

Snap snap.

CHAPTER 9

The two of us walked for about five minutes before we got out of the forest area and reached a park a few blocks away. There, Xavier took some food out of his leather jacket and handed some to me, followed by a can of soda.

"The breakfast of champions. Breakfast of criminals? Breakfast of creatures of lore on the run?" I tested out a few options, but none of them made Xavier laugh again. "I see. You only laugh when I get myself stuck in ridiculous situations. I'm starting to sense a pattern."

At least he cracked a smile at that. "You are something else, Cecilia Chevalier. The lady at the store said we were in a town called Somersville. Does that sound familiar to you?"

It did. "Yeah. Unfortunately, it means we didn't go too far. Only about an hour away from DeBruin. There should be a nice bookstore somewhere around here though. Miranda is always talking about it."

"Well... since you got a little nap and we're properly fed—" I snorted at that comment, "shall we?"

"Shall we what?"

"Find the bookstore?"

I blinked up at him as he stood, extending his hand down like he wanted me to take it and follow him. To a bookstore. In a random town. Like there weren't any other pressing worries at the moment.

"Xavier? Don't we have to, like, figure out our next step? How to stay away from the Fallere's? Find your mother?"

He grinned, and I watched as his canines ascended slightly into his mouth, giving him the illusion of a normal set of teeth, rather than vampire fangs. "I am not worried about my mother. Or yours," he added at the end. "And as long as we stay under the radar for a bit, keeping your magic at bay, then I'm not particularly worried about the circle either. Right now, as long as we're together, we'll be alright."

"Because we're fated," I tacked on, knowing what he meant.

But he shook his head. "No. Because you are Cecilia Chevalier. And I vowed to protect you at the cost of my own life, but the more I am learning about you, the more I'm realizing that *you* might be the one to protect us all."

I stopped walking then, dropping his hand. "What does that mean?"

"It means... you're new at this. And I've been around it my whole life, hearing stories, learning history, listening to elders speak of ancestors. Having you connect the stories about the fated lovers with Sonya and her protector made me realize just how similar their stories are with ours. And if you're anything like Sonya... we're going to be fine."

"As long as I don't get kidnapped." I wasn't sure if I meant it as a joke or not.

Xavier reached for my hand again, lifting it to his mouth and giving my knuckles a quick kiss. "Like I would ever let that happen."

"You know, when I first saw you at school the other week, I thought you were pompous, stuck up, and kind of rude."

"Did you? Because I thought you were annoying, obnoxious, and clueless."

My jaw dropped. "You did not."

Xavier shrugged. "I did. Obviously, I knew who you were, so I wasn't *too* judgmental against you. But... you were always getting yourself into trouble. You were foolish with your magic."

I knocked my shoulder into his, but he barely stumbled a foot. "Okay, you try and wake up one day with the ability to do this—"

With one glance over at the nearest store, I snapped, and all the shutters opened, the closed sign turning to open, and the lights going on inside. Then I snapped again, and it all returned to its original state.

"Fair. I know it's a big change. But you're handling it well. Well enough," he said, nudging me. He turned to me, his face becoming serious. "I am proud of you. It has to be hard, but you are doing so well, Cecilia. And above all, I thank you for placing your trust in me."

He leaned forward, brushing his lips gently across mine, like he once again was waiting for another invitation. When would this boy just use the confidence he had in every other part of his life and *kiss* me like he meant it?

"Xavier?" I whispered.

"Hmm?" He backed away only an inch.

"If you want to kiss me, then *kiss me*."

"My pleasure." He stepped forward, placing one foot between my legs, wrapped an arm around my waist, the other hand between my shoulder blades, and dipped me low. The ends of my hair brushed against the ground as Xavier lowered his head, capturing my lips with his, and did exactly as I asked.

I clung to his arms, but never felt as if I were to fall. He was strong, and like he said, I trusted him with my life. Literally. I knew he wouldn't let go of me, and he didn't.

Not after a minute. Not after he slowly raised me to my feet, and not after lifting his hands to both sides of my face, his cold fingers extinguishing the flames in my cheeks as he held me steady, kissing me until it felt like hours had passed.

"Next time, just start with that, huh?" I said breathlessly. The sun was up now, creating a cotton candy colored sky. There still wasn't anyone around, but I suspected someone would be coming by soon.

"I will never take you for granted Cecilia, and that means never assuming you want to kiss me unless you tell me so," Xavier said. "I don't want you to get the wrong idea—"

"It's only wrong if I don't feel the same way. Take this as your cue that I do. Everything you've done for me so far has been to help me. To protect me. To teach me. Minus the kidnapping. That... Well, you had good intentions, even if they were a bit out of line."

I had never seen his cheeks flush before, always staying the same pale skin, but I could have sworn the tiniest bit of pink appeared.

"I wouldn't have done it if—"

I put a finger on his lips and shushed him. "Nope. Right now, let's find that bookstore and wait until it opens."

Chapter 10

The wait was long. Much longer than I had patience for. Xavier was patient, though, mostly with me, as I fiddled with my magic. I asked him question after question, doing small parlor tricks in between answers.

I mostly asked him about his family, how he grew up, *where* he grew up, and all things vampire I didn't know. It didn't surprise me that most of it was actually like my life, minus the high school part. He said he never met my mother, but that was to keep her whereabouts safe. She didn't need Elodie at her side at all hours of the day like Xavier needed to be next to me right now. He also said that in time, I wouldn't need him as much either, after I learned more magic, and could protect and cloak myself easily.

When he said that, it felt like a knife severed my heart, twisting in deep to a spot I couldn't reach. I wanted to *snap* it away and stitch the heart back together, but I knew I couldn't. That had to be part of the fated love—never wanting to be away from the other.

Which was also something I would have to get used to. While I enjoyed people, and never felt overwhelmed by being surrounded, I could tell Xavier didn't feel the same. He was an introvert to my extrovert and it would take some time to get him to open up more.

With me, though, he seemed like an open book. There wasn't a question he didn't answer, although most of them were pretty surface level. Or maybe he was making up for all the questions he hadn't been able to answer. If I heard him say 'in due time,' I probably would have pushed him off of the bench we occupied.

"I wouldn't do much bigger than that," Xavier warned after I sent a squirrel flying from one tree to another.

"Because it'll set off alarm bells? How does that even work?" I let the squirrel free, and it scampered away.

"It's hard to explain, especially if you haven't been around other magic. The only time I was able to sense it was when I found you. Mother says she can sense if Celeste does something big, which isn't often, and only when she's aware no one is around."

"So I have to be close by?" I had so much to learn.

"Within a range. I am unsure what the range is, but even at the cemetery I could sense you doing magic in your home, and I'm only a vampire, not another witch."

That was frightening. Home was only a few blocks away, but if he could sense it there, then Ezra's mom probably had no issue from two houses down. Did she realize what it was she was feeling right away? Did she automatically assume it was me? They had been hiding out in DeBruin spying on my family for all these years after all.

Or was it when she heard Ezra use the word witch that she finally put the puzzle pieces together?

There would be some questions I would never know answers to. Hopefully, I would never run into Ezra's mother again...

Or Ezra.

That part hurt. Thinking about never seeing my best friend again tore at my heart, even with how he acted the other day. It had been such a flip, I wasn't sure I completely processed it all yet either.

We had been best friends. For years and years. He helped me through the start of finding out I had magic to begin with, with almost no questions asked.

Then, things started getting weird. He distanced himself while also becoming almost more protective of me. Now I knew it had something to do with his mother, but I didn't know that at first.

After that came the love confession. The kiss. Thinking back, it almost felt like one last plea to save him. To save us. What would have happened if I had told him I loved him back? If I had kissed him back? Would it have changed anything? Would he have let his mother tell him such horrible things about me and my family, my circle?

Would he have attacked me and tried to take my magic?

I knew the ring had something to do with it. The way his eyes flashed red before he lunged at me. That wasn't Ezra. That wasn't my best friend in there.

If I ever saw him again, and I got the ring of–

"Cecilia?" Xavier's voice cut through my thoughts. "The bookshop is open."

I looked up, finding him standing in front of me waiting, the door to the bookstore propped open across the street behind him.

"What are the chances they have old research texts about magical families at war?" I asked, slipping my hand into his as we walked across the empty street.

"Probably zero, but never say never."

It wasn't quite the question I wanted to ask the employee when we walked in, so we just shared greetings and started to browse.

Xavier went off to the non-fiction aisle, looking at books on ancient philosophers, while I veered more toward fantasy and paranormal novels. They weren't my normal genre, but I figured if all fiction was rooted in some sort of fact, then maybe I could learn more about witches and vampires there.

The shelves were high, the rows were long, and before I knew it, I had gotten lost within the store and time. I patted my jeans, hoping to have remembered at least one thing, and groaned when I realized my phone was not with me. I had no idea what time it was. I had no connection to anyone except Xavier. I couldn't text Miranda or Matt, not that I could tell them what was going on even if I could.

I wondered if Ezra was still in DeBruin, if he went to school today, if he spoke with my friends. Would he try to brainwash them into ratting me out? Maybe it was a good thing I couldn't contact anyone. Elodie said they wouldn't hurt Gramps, but what if they suspected he knew where I was?

I grabbed another book from the shelf and opened it, finding a gruesome illustration of a vampire popping out at me. It took me by surprise, then I let out a small huff of laughter. The vampires I knew, all two of them, looked nothing like that. Xavier didn't wear a long, black, high-necked cape. He wore black shirts and a black leather jacket. They didn't have such pale skin it was almost translucent or completely blood-red lips. And neither Xavier nor Elodie allowed their canines to protrude past their lips and hang out of their mouths. They only forced them out when needed, like when Xavier had to fight Ezra.

Or when he had to convince me that vampires were real to begin with.

"Hey, Xavier, you should—" I spun around to find him, but before I could finish, I ran into someone in front of me. "I'm sorry, I—"

My breath caught in my throat. A girl stood there, staring back at me with wide, green eyes. She blinked, her lips parting slightly as she took me in.

I did the same, because it was like looking in a mirror.

Chapter 11

"Are… are…" the girl cleared her throat, finally breaking away from staring in my eyes and glancing down at my outfit. My purple sweater seemed like a massively bright color compared to her cream colored one. "Are you Cecilia?"

My brows furrowed. How did she know my name? And why did she look exactly like me? From the rusty auburn hair down to the high cheekbones and freckles scattered across my nose, she was almost identical to me in every way except height. Where I wasn't gifted in the vertical position, she was even less so, about three inches shorter than me.

"Who are you?" I asked, slowly returning the book to the shelf without taking my eyes off of her. For some reason, I wanted to pull her into a hug and never let go. She had one of those faces that just made you love her instantly, a soft, innocent face. While our features were the same, she was much more naïve looking than I was, like she hadn't gone through many hardships in life.

Not that I had, in the greater sense of things, but her… she was almost angelic. Her green eyes, like mine, had a little shimmer to them.

"Cecilia Chevalier?" she clarified. I nodded, still unsure what was happening.

Then, in a blink, she lifted her hand and snapped twice.

"May I see that necklace?" she asked with a slight waver in her voice, like it terrified her to say.

My hand flew to my throat, grasping at the charm. "This one? Of course. It's beautiful, isn't it? I think it would look amazing on you. Why don't you try it on?"

I lifted it over my head and put it around hers in a flash. Instead of smiling, though, she looked upset by the move.

"I'm sorry, he made me—"

"Hey, CC. I've been looking for you."

I grinned wide, startling the girl. Her eyes darted back and forth between me and the person behind me.

"Ezra! I'm so glad to see you!" I said, turning around and throwing my arms around his neck. He wrapped his around my back, patting me a few times, holding me to him.

"Me too, CC. Me too. Hey, want to grab a coffee? There's a cute little café down the street," he said after letting me go.

"Yes! Oh my gosh, we have so much to catch up on! Have you met—" I paused, realizing I hadn't gotten the name of the girl who looked exactly like me.

"Amara. Yes, we've met. She's coming too. It was very generous of you to show her your necklace." Ezra grabbed both of our hands and led us out of the bookstore.

There was a nagging in the back of my mind, like I had forgotten something. Had I put the book I was looking at back on the shelf? Or was I going to buy it? Which one was it again? Something to do with... ghosts? Werewolves?

I couldn't remember, but it was alright. Maybe after coffee we could come back and I could buy it then. Ezra loved bookstores, after all. The main reason I usually went to them was because of him or Miranda.

His grip on my hand tightened as we walked down the block. I noticed he did the same on Amara's hand as well.

"How do you two know each other? Isn't it crazy, Ez, she looks just like me!" I smiled at Amara, hoping to calm her down. She looked rather worried and worked up for some reason.

"Oh, we just met. She's very nice, even doing me a favor."

"What's that? Hey, wait, why are you in Somersville? Aren't you supposed to be at school? Your mom is going to be *pissed* if you skip again, Ezra! She already forbade you from seeing me once. We really shouldn't push our luck."

Ezra shook his head. "No, it's fine. She knows where I am. Actually, she sent me to get you."

"To... get me? For what?"

"We have big plans for you, CC. For you *and* Amara. You'll see soon." He stared me in the eyes for a moment, and I could have sworn I saw a flash of red behind those big, dark frames of his.

Amara whimpered next to Ezra, and I frowned again. What was he talking about and why did it seem to upset Amara so much?

Also... why was Ezra allowed to touch her while she was wearing the necklace? Hadn't his touch burned me any time he tried while I had it on?

"Ezra... where are we going?" We had been walking for a while now, and there was no coffee shop in sight. My head began to pound. He had said coffee, right?

Suddenly, it felt like my mind was pushed up against a brick wall. What happened at the bookstore? I was looking at a book and then... then...

I grimaced, the pain deepening. Then, my right hand heated up, starting at my finger and spreading into my arm. The hand that wasn't holding on to Ezra. I shook it off trying to get it to stop, but it wouldn't.

What was happening? I looked down, finding a ring on my finger glowing. It wasn't super bright, but still shone down on the sidewalk, the warmth traveling up my arm and into my shoulder.

My eyes grew wide. Something was happening. Ezra was muttering to himself, so I looked behind him, over at Amara. She saw my worry and nodded, mouthing something, but I couldn't make out what it was.

She repeated it over and over, until it finally clicked.

Snap.

She wanted me to snap? Like to a beat? But there was no music.

Her arm swung behind her, slightly past what was normal for a hurried walk. I glanced at it, finding her holding up two fingers, then miming snapping.

Twice. She wanted me to snap twice. But why? Was she about to break out into song and dance? Were we going to start a round?

"Bring them to the park. Bring them to the park," Ezra muttered under his breath.

"The park? I thought we were going to get coffee?" I said, but something out of the corner of my eye caught my attention.

Amara shook her head, her face stern. She mouthed the words again, *snap snap snap snap*, so fast this time I almost couldn't make out when one word ended and the other began.

Fine. If that's what she wanted, then fine.

She flashed me two fingers again, over and over behind her back.

Ezra tugged at our hands, pulling us back so we were walking in sync with him. It was now or never.

I twisted my hand behind my back and placed my thumb against my middle finger.

Snap snap.

Instantly, my ring heated so much, I almost ripped it off and threw it. It burned through my hand, my entire body boiling.

Ezra dropped my other hand in a flash, shaking his like he, too, had been burned. He turned toward me, his mouth agape.

"Again!" Amara cried. Ezra still had her in a hold and pulled her closer as she screamed.

Snap snap.

In a heartbeat, she disappeared, only to reappear by my side a second later.

"You traitor! You know what will happen now!" Ezra screeched. Amara shook as she stood behind me. I blocked her as much as I could.

Snap snap.

I wasn't sure why I was still snapping, but it seemed to be the right thing to do. Ezra froze in place, his arm outstretched as he had started to reach for Amara, but I stopped him before he could get there. I kept a hand on Amara's arm, just to make sure she was safe.

Then, in one swift movement, I grabbed the ring off of Ezra's hand and threw it to the ground.

Snap snap.

The ring burst into flames, dissolving into ash on the sidewalk.

"Here! You need this," Amara cried, reaching up and taking the necklace off of her neck. I looped it around mine and grabbed her hand just as a bright red flash streaked past the both of us.

"Ezra! Grab them!" a familiar voice shouted.

The park. We were at the edge of the park, the same one Xavier and I had appeared in hours earlier.

They must have traced my magic here, the more powerful witches in the circle able to track us an hour away.

"Amara, we don't have time to figure this out, but how powerful is your magic?"

"You mean the snapping thing? I don't know, but I've done some really weird stuff with it." Her voice shook again. She was terrified, as was I.

"Ezra!"

My spell didn't last long enough. Ezra broke through the freeze a second later, stumbling forward with the momentum he had prior to stopping. Amara and I took a step back, out of his way, watching him tumble to the ground next to the pile of ashes where his ring used to be.

"Ezra now!"

He looked up, and our eyes connected. His flickered with a hint of a red ring, then died down to the amber they used to be. They softened, a frown replacing the sneer from a moment ago.

"CC?"

My heart plummeted. Ezra. *My* Ezra was back.

"Ezra! Ezra you have to leave—" I stopped myself. Where was he going to go? What would he do? It wasn't like he had another family to join or somewhere safe to go.

"I'm so sorry, Ezra. You were my best friend. I hope your family reminds you that you're loved no matter what. Because I loved you. So much." I stroked his cheek and he leaned into my hand.

"What's going on? Who is that? Where are we?"

"It's a long story, Ez, and I don't have time to explain. But remember—if your mother asks you to wear a ring, say no. Say no as long as you are able. Remember me. Remember us. Say no while remembering how much you love me and how amazing of a best friend you were to me."

Another bright red streak passed by us. I barely flinched this time, but Ezra ducked down to the sidewalk. I grabbed his arms and hefted him to his feet.

"Cecilia!"

Xavier flew between me and Ezra, knocking him to the ground once more. Faster than I could blink, he hauled Ezra into the air, preparing to toss him again. Xavier had Ezra by the throat mid-air, Ezra's eyes wide with terror.

"Xavier, no!"

CHAPTER 12

X avier paused, only long enough to look back at me. His canines were descended, his brows furrowed. He was... frightening. But the look on my face must have been enough to stop him. "No, Xavier, you can't."

He lowered a panicked looking Ezra to his feet and turned to me. "What happened? Are you alright?"

I pointed down to the sidewalk, showing him the pile of ashes. "I got his ring. I burned it. I think... I think Ezra is back. Like normal. Not a hunter."

"You... you *burned* it? That's not possible. That's the ring of the hunters. It's unable to be damaged."

I shrugged. "Well, I damaged it pretty good."

One more streak flew, this time hitting Amara in the shoulder. She spun, her arms flailing out to the sides. Xavier flashed over, catching her before she hit the ground.

"CC? Who is that?" Ezra sounded panicked now, like he did when he forgot to study for a mid-term once. "And how did *he* just do *that*?" It was like he knew nothing from post-Xavier times. Did he not remember the cemetery? The night before, in his backyard? What did he know?

I turned. "I'm so sorry, Ezra, but I can't explain. Maybe one day I can." Tears streamed down my cheeks, my heart shattering at the loss.

"Cecilia, we need to leave," Xavier urged, holding a limp Amara in his arms and looking down at me. "Now."

"But if they found me here, then—"

"Further. We have to go further. Hold her hand and snap. You can do it. I know you can." He shifted Amara in his arms and grabbed me around the waist, leaning down and kissed me with the passion I told him never to waver on again. Ezra groaned behind me, but I paid him no attention. I held Xavier's arm with my left hand, pressed my lips into his, and raised my right hand.

Snap snap.

I was going to throw up. I really, really wanted to throw up. My insides felt like they were on the outside and my head detached from my body.

"Ugh," someone next to me groaned. "I think I'm going to be sick."

I couldn't get the world to stop spinning long enough to look over. I squeezed my eyes shut, swallowing down whatever had risen into my throat.

An icy cold hand laid over my forehead, pressing into my temples, instantly settling my dizziness and my stomach. The hand disappeared, and the sound of relief from the person next to me hit my ears.

"Cecilia." Xavier returned to me, sitting behind me and gently lifting my torso. I wasn't quite ready to sit on my own, though, so he stretched his long legs out next to mine and laid me on his chest, allowing my head to fall backwards onto his shoulder. "You did it, Cecilia," he whispered directly into my ear. "You saved us."

"Isn't that your job?"

I didn't have to see him to know he was grinning. Instead of answering, he leaned down and kissed me so gently, it felt like butterflies wings brushing against my lips.

But it also set my heart on fire.

"Cecilia?" A soft, lithe voice said next to me. I peeked one eye open to see my doppelgänger struggling to sit up.

Xavier reached out, steadying her while never letting me fall. Such a gentleman, he was.

"I'm so sorry, Cecilia. That... that guy, Ezra?"

I nodded, confirming his name. It was obvious that she hadn't known him like Ezra had mentioned he did.

"He found me in the park earlier. I was going for a walk, to the coffee shop actually, and he called me your name, Cecilia. When I didn't answer, he grabbed me and... and... I don't know what happened, actually. It felt like I was dying from the inside out. Then he told me to find you and bring you to him. If I didn't, he would continue what he was doing until I was dead."

Xavier stiffened behind me. "Ezra is a hunter."

Amara scrunched her cute little nose. "What does that mean?"

Slowly, we both turned to look directly at her. I blinked, shellshocked.

"Amara... you're a witch."

"I know *that*."

"What circle do you belong in?" Xavier asked, one hand clutching at my hip like he was holding me in place. Or maybe he was holding himself back.

"Circle? I don't know what you mean."

"Who taught you your magic?"

Amara's face fell. "Oh. My mother. She passed away a few weeks ago, though. Just a few days after my eighteenth birthday. It was so sudden. Some illness that just took the life out of her. Her doctor said she'd never seen anything like it."

"Was it like... like the life had been drained out of her?" I whispered, desperately wanting Amara to say it wasn't.

But she nodded, fiddling with a blade of grass underneath her leg. "Yeah. I brought her to the hospital because she could barely walk. Once the doctor came in, it was only hours before she was gone."

"What was the doctor's last name? Was there a male doctor?" Xavier's questions seemed odd for Amara, but I followed his train of thought.

"I'll never forget it. It was a lady named Doctor Fallere, and a man named Doctor Mortis."

My head fell back onto Xavier's shoulder again as I cried out. "Amara, I'm so sorry."

"Can someone please tell me what's going on?"

"Your mother was drained. Of her magic," Xavier said in the gentle way that made it seem like whatever he was saying wasn't the most horrible thing ever. Between his accent and his cadence, it was soothing, even though his words hit hard like a knife to the gut. "The male was a hunter, and the female doctor a witch of a powerful circle. The one we saw back there. The male though..." he trailed off.

"What is it?" I questioned him, leaving Amara still gaping.

"Mortis. It's another circle. If the Fallere and the Mortis circles are working together... and against your family... It's worse than we thought." Xavier grimaced, like he hated telling me that fact just as much as I hated hearing it.

There was nothing I could do about that information now though, so I turned back to Amara to clue her in. "Ezra was my best friend for years. Until I developed my magic and his family found out, turning him into a hunter seemingly overnight. Hunters go out and drain the magic from powerful witches in circles that they deem have 'too much power.'" I was proud of myself for being able to answer questions finally, even if they weren't the ones I wanted to answer.

"Why would they take my mother?" Amara cried, tears streaming down her cheeks.

I sat up now, a newfound energy surging through me. "Because... you look like me. That's my guess, anyway."

"And that's bad?"

"Well, it's probably not good. I'm assuming we're related somehow. Do you know anything about your ancestors?"

"Mom told me once. There was Mom, grandma, her grandma, everyone's mothers and grandmothers." Amara scrunched her face in thought. "All the way back to some woman named Seraphine."

"That's impossible." Xavier tucked his feet in, but stayed next to me, one arm on my lower back to support me.

"No, pretty sure it was someone named Seraphine."

I glanced over at Xavier. "I mean, she looks almost exactly like me. It seems possible."

"Yeah, I mean, I'm shorter, but otherwise we're pretty close. The weird thing would be if you have one of these." Amara lifted her left arm and pushed down her sweater a few inches, showing a faded scar on her wrist.

I couldn't believe what I was seeing. Not only did this girl look identical to me, but she had the same weird scar on her wrist.

"Cecilia? Are you alright? Breathe, Cecilia, breathe." Xavier's hand rubbed at my back as he waved a hand in front of my face.

Wordlessly, I lifted my left arm and pulled back my shirt sleeve, revealing my scar. To me, it looked like an elongated S stretched horizontally, with an extra hook at the bottom jutting to the left. I asked Gramps about it once, but he never had an answer for me. He didn't know what it could have been from and said I must have been born with it.

"Where did you get that?" Xavier exclaimed, grabbing my wrist and holding it closer to his face. Then he did the same with Amara's arm, holding both of our wrists side by side.

They were identical.

"What do you know?" I asked him. His eyes were wild as he looked back between the two.

"We have to find my mother. As soon as possible."

CHAPTER 13

I t took a few hours to locate exactly where we were. Mostly, because it turned out we weren't in the same country anymore. Xavier was skilled with languages, yet even he was having a hard time figuring out the road signs we managed to find after walking for an hour.

"You snapped us to Europe?" Amara asked in awe. "All I could do was snap some cookies from the pantry or make something accidentally explode."

"It was partly because of you. I probably couldn't have done it had we not been holding hands. How long have you had your magic?" I asked, walking quietly behind Xavier.

"Less than a month. When I turned eighteen in mid-October. Mom was nervous at first, then told me little bits here and there. She tried to help me, but then... Well..."

I didn't want to subject her to thinking about her mother passing away again, so I moved on. "Do you have a vampire protector?"

Amara shook her head. "Mother said she did, when she was younger, but not anymore."

"But not you? Why not you? Why wasn't one called to you when you developed your magic?"

"Vampire protectors aren't all the same," Xavier interrupted. "Some families deny theirs, thinking they're safe in this day and age."

"What about the 'if I die, you die' clause?"

Amara gasped, covering her face. "He'll *die* if you die?"

Xavier stopped walking and turned toward both of us. "Like I said, some vampire families take their jobs more seriously than others. Especially if they're bound to a more powerful circle..."

"But Amara is in our circle."

The look on Xavier's face said it all. Family circles had many branches from witches making families of their own. Even though we both descended from Seraphine, we could still be fourth cousins seventeen times removed or something.

"Mother will have answers. She's probably with your mother now," Xavier said, turning back to the road and continuing to walk.

"That's dangerous, though, isn't it? We were supposed to avoid finding my mother or else they could find us."

Xavier reached back for my hand, pulling me up to meet him shoulder to shoulder. He lifted my hand and kissed my knuckles. "Three makes a circle, Cecilia. You. Your mother. Amara. And with the magic you just used to transport us to a different *country*... Well, it's safe to say they're already hunting us. The sooner we find your mother and mine, the sooner we're in a safer location, hidden."

"Hidden. I feel like all I do is hide."

Xavier let out a laugh at that.

"What? It's the truth! I hid from you for eighteen years!"

"Cecilia, your name *means* hidden. It means blind, or to hide, in Latin. Amara means everlasting."

"My middle name means powerful," Amara offered, joining the conversation.

Xavier frowned. "What is your middle name?"

"Potentia. It's weird, I think it's unique. Mom never said, but I always thought it was probably a—"

"Family name," I finished for her. I squeezed Xavier's hand, now realizing the urgency. "We have to find Mom."

"Everlasting power and hidden power," Xavier chuckled to himself. "You know Latin, Amara?"

"Just names, mostly. It was a hobby."

"What does Celeste mean?" I blurted out, wanting to know if Mom had something like ours.

"Heavenly. Like celestial."

"And Collette?" Might as well go for all the family members, even Gramma.

Amara thought for a moment. "It's not really Latin based, but..."

"It's derived from Nicolaus, or Nicole," Xavier said, prompting her like he already knew the answer but wanted to give her a chance.

Amara brightened at that. "Oh! Then it means victory for the people."

"Everlasting power. Hidden power. Heavenly power. Victory for the people," I muttered to myself. "Our family is quite literal."

"Indeed. But, within circles, names have power themselves. There's a reason that some are handed down and repeated..." Xavier stopped to read another road sign, then took us to the left. Hopefully we would reach somewhere soon because I was *starving*. Teleporting three people to another country really did a number on the appetite.

"Like Potentia," I whispered, unsure if Amara heard me.

She did. She looked over at me, her angelic eyes wide. It almost made me laugh because of how much she looked like *me* made me wonder if this was the look Ezra saw from me so often. "Is your middle name Potentia too?"

I tapped my finger to my nose. "Bingo. And my mom's. And my grandmothers."

"Stems from Seraphine Potentia," Xavier threw in. "Look, we're here."

"Where is *here*, exactly?"

He just shrugged. "Somewhere with food and a map, I hope. If we can locate ourselves on the map, then I can figure out how far we need to go to get to Mother."

"You had me at food."

Amara and I stuffed ourselves while he tried to speak with the shop owner. He thankfully took whatever money Xavier and Amara had in their pockets, obviously sensing that we were desperate. Amara and I could have snapped him into a daze or snapped some food into our pockets, but we weren't like that. Tricking the nurse to let me leave school early was one thing; blatant stealing in a foreign country would have been going too far.

"Good news," Xavier said as he returned to us. I uncapped a bottle of water and slid it over to him along with a turkey and cheese sandwich. He took a swig and a bite, then continued. "We're one country away."

I blinked, almost choking on my own sandwich. "What? I really got us that close without even knowing?"

"Closer than you think. The border is only about ten kilometers away." Xavier gave me a beaming smile, his canines protruding slightly, like he was so happy he couldn't even control it.

"Way to go, Cecilia!" Amara said, leaning over to give me a high five.

We gulped down the rest of our food and headed back outside, to the deserted streets. Xavier produced a map the shopkeeper also graciously had given him, and pointed to our destination.

"I've never been there, so I won't be able to tell you if we're right or wrong until we can locate one of our mothers."

"One of them? Won't your mom be with mine?" I questioned, looking at him in worry. Elodie said she would be with Mom. She said it before we left.

Xavier nodded slowly and patted my arm. "Yes, but also no. From what I know, she has a separate residence about an hour away from your mother. Just close enough where your mother can call for her without revealing too much magic, yet far enough where it won't give her location away."

I let out a long breath. "Wow. Thought of everything to keep Mom hidden. Maybe her name should have been Cecilia."

Amara cleared her throat, and we both turned to her. "Sorry, but... *why* is your mother hidden? And how are we going to find them? Walking around for hours on end?"

"Cecilia and I will be able to sense when we get close to our mothers," Xavier said, not answering the first question.

Since I wasn't super sure of the right answer myself, I didn't either. Instead, I held out one hand, grabbed onto Amara's, then wound my other arm around Xavier's waist, keeping my right hand free.

Snap snap.

CHAPTER 19

The sensation of flying through the air uncontrollably didn't sit as well with me for the third time.

This time, I actually vomited.

Amara, too. We both leaned over, retching as soon as we landed. Or fell. Or whatever it was we did.

Xavier seemed to hold his own, however. "Cecilia? Cecilia, are you alright?"

I wiped my mouth with the back of my hand and laid back down on my back, giving my stomach time to settle.

"Next time, I vote for a train or something," Amara whispered, adding a groan at the end. I wanted to vocalize my agreement, but I didn't know what would happen if I opened my mouth.

"Cecilia?" There was urgency in Xavier's tone. It got me to open my eyes and stare up at him, since he was hovering over my face. I grimaced, not wanting him to be so close to my vomit breath.

Could I... Instead of spending time wondering, I just did it.

Snap snap.

"Ohhhh," Amara sighed. "Whatever that was, thank you."

Instantly, I felt better too. It was a risky move, but somehow, I knew it would work.

Before I could sit up, though, I felt it. A new feeling flowing through me. It wasn't the same as the tingle, the hum, or even the deep shiver I used to get from Xavier.

This was different. This felt like... home. Comfort. Of chocolate chip cookies straight from the oven. Of Gramma's hugs, of her stroking my hair when I was upset. Of security and joy.

"Mom," I whispered. "I feel it."

Xavier took my hands and lifted me to my feet, then turned to help Amara. "I feel it too. If I had to guess, our mothers are together. And they're close."

"How do we find them from here?" If Mom had been hidden, even from Xavier, then we were helpless. Unless we hung around long enough for Elodie to find us, but who knew how long that could take.

Xavier closed his eyes and reached for my hand. The moment we interlaced our fingers, the feeling grew significantly stronger.

And it pulled me forward, as if by an invisible string.

"Forward it is," Amara whispered, a small grin on her face as she followed behind.

My heart reached for her. Here Xavier and I were, ready to be reunited with our mothers, while hers had been taken from her at such a young age.

"I never met my mom," I told her, looping my other arm through hers. "She left me with my grandparents the day I was born and took off. She's been in hiding ever since, most likely from the Fallere circle, among others."

Amara's eyes widened, and it was then that I realized again how similar we really were. Not just in looks, but in that scar on our wrists too.

"Xavier? The scars? What do they mean?"

But he kept staring straight ahead, as if he thought our moms would pop up out of the ground and didn't answer.

I leaned into Amara and said, "He does that sometimes. Not too big on answering questions right away."

She giggled and reached down to hold my hand. I had hers in my left, Xavier's in my right, the ring on my index finger growing warmer with each step, and the necklace on my chest doing the same. I took it to mean we were on the right path, and getting close.

A few minutes later, Xavier stopped. He pointed at a large gate about a block ahead.

"Seriously? Another cemetery? My mother has been hiding in a cemetery this whole time?" Back when I joked with Elodie about staying in one forever, she made it seem like it was possible. But I hadn't taken her *seriously*. "Poor Mom..."

Xavier smirked, like he knew something I didn't. Then, he spilled. "If we're in the right spot, and I believe we are, then I have no doubt your mother has an amazing home somewhere inside. She's not living in a mausoleum, I guarantee you."

That lifted my spirits a bit. "So... Can we just walk right though? I know I had to go through a lot of things first..."

"Mother will meet us at the gates. She'll bring us through." The confidence had returned to Xavier's voice, which made me feel stronger too.

A moment later, the three of us stood, hand in hand, waiting. The minutes ticked by, yet Elodie didn't show.

"Um..." I started, but Xavier squeezed my hand, silencing me.

We waited some more, until I got so antsy, I couldn't stand it.

"Xavier. How would they know we're here?"

"The same way we knew where they were."

"Yeah, but your mom said magic couldn't be detected within the protected areas, like the cemetery back home. What if they can't feel us from the inside?"

Xavier set his jaw and furrowed his brows, clearly frustrated with me. This time, I was going to take it into my own hands.

Dropping his, I also let go of Amara's, knowing that we worked bigger magic together, and concentrated on the gates.

Snap snap.

"Cecilia!" Xavier exclaimed through gritted teeth. A second later, though, the gates swung open just enough to let us through.

"Low level magic can't be detected. Besides, it's not like Ezra traveled all the way to Europe with us," I retorted, wanting to break out into a smile at my genius, but keeping it to myself instead.

"It's not just the Fallere's, and not all of them live in DeBruin, you know." He took hold of my hand again and walked toward the gates.

I reached back and grabbed Amara, who stumbled as she stared wide-eyed at the whole situation.

The second Xavier led us through the gates, I felt it. The pull. The comfort. The overwhelming sensation of *home*.

"Mom," I whispered. "She's here."

"She's waiting for you," a sweet, lithe voice said from behind us.

Amara practically jumped out of her skin and whirled around.

Elodie tripped over her own feet, taking a few steps back as she looked at Amara, then to me, and back to Amara. "What... Who... Xavier, what has happened?"

Xavier, still clutching my hand like a life preserver, stepped forward. "Mother, this is Amara. We met her at the town Cecilia snapped us to first. There, we ran into Ezra and the Fallere's, before Cecilia and Amara combined their magic and snapped us over here. They're strong, Mother. And then there's this..."

Xavier pointed to my wrist, and I immediately turned it over to show Elodie the scar. I nudged Amara, who still stood looking completely shell shocked, then she did the same.

Elodie's jaw fell open. Her chest heaved as she looked at our identical markings.

"That's not all..." Xavier pulled his shirt down and showed his mother the symbol of the medallion on his chest. I, not wanting to move my sweater, patted my chest as well.

Xavier's mother looked about ready to lose her mind, which was fair. If things hadn't happened so fast lately, I would probably have done the same.

"Fated love bonds? That hasn't been seen in... centuries. Not since..." Elodie seemed at a loss for words, so I jumped in.

"Since Sonya?"

"And Julian," another voice said from behind us.

This time, I whirled around and almost fell over at the sight.

Mom.

Chapter 15

Though I had never met her, I would recognize her anywhere.

Mainly because she looked just like me. And Amara. Just in
between our heights, with a few more wrinkles at the corner of
her eyes, and a softer smile like she was expecting us, yet was
surprised to see there were two girls.

"Cecilia," she reached toward me, taking my hands in hers.
"I'm so glad you're here." She pulled me in for a hug and instantly I felt at ease.

"You hug like Gramps," I whispered into her ear. "Gramps
says he loves you, by the way."

She sniffled, but didn't break apart for another full minute or
two. "I miss him dearly." Then, she turned toward Amara.

"And my beautiful Amara." Mom reached out her hands to
take Amara's, but didn't pull her in for the same hug.

"Celeste..." Elodie didn't have to ask the full question for all
of us to understand what she meant.

How did Mom know Amara?

"Please. Let's get settled. No need for proper introductions
and storytelling while standing out here."

Xavier was right. Mom had a wonderful little cottage in the
back of the cemetery, away from gravestones and mausoleums.
There were two small bedrooms, a kitchen, and a living space. A
massive bookshelf covered one wall of the living room. A couch

with a small window were on the other. It was warm, cozy, and just what we all needed.

After Elodie put on a kettle, Amara, Xavier, and I settled in with some food, and Mom sat at a chair at the small table.

"I bet you all have questions. I have the answers, so maybe I should start?" Mom asked, but no one needed to answer.

"Since I've been here for so many years, I've done more research than a normal person would probably ever do. I've found many things that I'm assuming not a lot of people know. Starting with, centuries ago, Sonya Potentia was one of the strongest witches our circle had ever seen. Her and her twin sister Seraphine were inseparable. They were fraternal, but looked almost identical. Sonya was paired with a vampire named Julian. She had him make a protection medallion, which she spelled. Then they fell in love, and her medallion symbol burned onto her wrist."

I turned to Amara as Mom paused. "I'll catch you up on the specifics later," I whispered. She nodded, but was otherwise entirely transfixed on Mom, just like I was.

"Sonya and Julian were fated loves. Not the first, but the strongest. And the last," she added at the end. "Until, seemingly, the two of you." Mom looked between Xavier and I with a knowing glance. Xavier had sat next to me on the couch, Amara on my other side. He held my hand in his, resting on top of his knee. He had barely let me out of his sight much less let me go since the moment we left Somerville.

"There's one piece of information that has not been widely spread throughout the circle, though. One piece purposefully left out of all records, even oral histories. Sonya's kidnapping."

All eyes snapped to her now. Even Elodie stopped making tea for a moment and stared at Mom wide-eyed. "Celeste?"

Whatever Mom was about to say looked like it was a surprise to Elodie as well.

Mom nodded and gave her a pitiful look. "I'm so sorry, El. But the truth is, Sonya wasn't kidnapped. At the last second, Seraphine cast a powerful cloaking spell, making herself look like Sonya. When the Fallere's found out weeks later, they drained her out of retaliation and spite."

I gasped. "That means…"

The look on Mom's face turned to sorrow. "Sonya was pregnant. Seraphine sacrificed herself to save her sister. Afterwards, Sonya, still cloaked as Seraphine, obviously couldn't be seen with Julian. So she went into hiding. The circle said it was because she couldn't handle the loss of her sister, but really, they couldn't risk exposing the secret to everyone. The Fallere's kept up the charade of having Sonya, though they said through marriage. They still wanted her and didn't want to tell the world they kidnapped the wrong sister. But they didn't know about that—" Mom pointed to my wrist. I rubbed it, suddenly a little self-conscious about the scar.

"They didn't know Sonya had a fated love. Eventually, our circle got Julian to Sonya, and their story has a happier ending than Seraphine's. Although Sonya kept up the look of her sister for the rest of her life, so everyone descended assumes they are Seraphine's descendants."

"But… that means we're descended from Sonya," I stated, cringing with the obviousness.

"Yes, dear. And it seems you share a *lot* with Sonya Potentia. Not just a name." She grinned. "You, Cecilia Chevalier, have a fated love, just like her. That scar on your wrist? Is the symbol from Sonya's medallion. Not unlike the one you have, that I assume is now scarred onto your chests?" She looked at my medallion, hanging around my neck from the chain.

Xavier pulled his shirt aside and showed Mom the mark. She nodded, as if expecting it.

"From my research, the symbol on your wrists," she gestured to both me and Amara, "has never been seen on a witch before, outside of Sonya herself."

All the air left my lungs. This was getting weirder and weirder by the second. I glanced over at Amara, trying to see how she was taking it all. I had to bite back a small laugh when I found her sitting so stiffly, her eyes wide and unblinking, almost as if she were a statue.

I was glad to know she was taking it as well as I was...

Mom continued. "And you have a twin. No other family line in our circle has had twins since Sonya and Seraphine, two of the most powerful witches ever to live."

My jaw *dropped*. Elodie and Xavier had mentioned I was rather powerful for my age and experience, but this?

I was basically Sonya reincarnated. As was Amara, except for the fated love part.

"Twins. Each born bearing the mark of Sonya Potentia. The moment I saw, I had a decision to make. I couldn't let them find you, not both of you." Mom looked at Amara directly now. Elodie dropped into a chair next to Mom, leaving the tea behind. "The Fallere's and their ancestors have been searching for witches in our line for centuries. If they knew I had twins, much less ones bearing the mark of Sonya Potentia, the two of you would be dead before you had the chance to live. I wouldn't do that to you. I couldn't."

Tears welled up in her eyes as she tried to blink them back. Then, she turned her attention to Amara.

"Amara Potentia, I am so sorry. I left you in the most capable hands I knew. Your mother was a very distant cousin, one I only knew of by name, one I knew had turned away her vampire protector, who lived a life away from the circle, without use of magic. I thought it best for you, to grow up outside of the world we lived in, the world that threatened us constantly. If you did, maybe you wouldn't develop your magic. You would be *safe*."

"I... You're... We're... What?" Amara stuttered.

"I am your mother by birth. But please, do not misunderstand me. Your mother was your mother in every way possible. She raised you, she loved you, she—"

"*Died* for me. For this," Amara waved her hand around toward all of us. "She *died*."

Mom's face paled. Elodie's hand flew over her own mouth. Neither of them knew.

"I think we need to back up a little," I interrupted. Neither Mom nor Elodie knew what happened to us once we left home. They needed to catch up before Mom kept going.

So, I told them. I told Mom how my powers developed. I told her all about Ezra and how he was my best friend in the world, how he was doing research. Innocent research, at first.

Then I told her about meeting Xavier. How he protected me from the moment we first met.

I continued on with Ezra, the attack, the cemetery, leaving Gramps' house, finding Amara, and defeating Ezra.

"They found you?" Mom asked, directing her question at Amara. "This is my fault. Had I told someone, *anyone*, about you, you would have had your own vampire protector—"

"She would have had Xavier. Amara developed her abilities first," Elodie said, a rather strict tone in her voice, like a principal disciplining a student.

Xavier sat rigid next to me, his hand tightening over mine. I didn't dare look at him, already unable to stomach the thought.

"If you had told us about her, Celeste, she would have had protection from the start. Ezra and the Fallere's wouldn't have been able to find her, much less drain her mother and almost her."

Mom didn't seem fazed by Elodie's harsh words. Instead, she looked defeated. Like she knew it was her fault, and was beating herself up inside over it. I opened my mouth to say something, but paused as a thought came over me first. When we arrived at the cemetery, Mom didn't look all that surprised to see Amara.

So I asked. "When we stood there in the cemetery... you looked as if you almost expected to see Amara. Me, sure. Elodie probably told you everything that happened up until we left. But why didn't you seem surprised to see her?"

Mom's green eyes shifted over to me, a small smile spreading across her lips. It was uncanny, watching her expressions match mine, match Amara's. It was like there were three clones in one room, with slight, tiny differences.

"I expected it. Once Elodie said you developed your powers, I knew it was only time before Amara did. Or, potentially had already. And once that happened, you would be bound to find each other."

I sighed. More vague answers. Though it made some sense, I knew it wasn't the whole story.

"Let me just recap everything that's gone on so far here," I said, wanting to make sure I was up to date. "Amara and I are twins."

Mom nodded. "Fraternal, but almost identical. Just like Sonya and Seraphine."

"The first twins born in the circle since those two," I clarified. She nodded again. Elodie sat behind her, still looking like she was in massive shock at all the news.

The only person who hadn't moved a muscle was Xavier. He sat perfectly still, his fingers interlaced with mine, as if he were absorbing all the information through me.

"And because of that, and these scars, you think we're just as powerful as they were?"

That's where Mom stopped me. "No, Cecilia. I think the two of you might be *more* powerful. Especially after what Elodie has told me about what you've been able to do, in such a short time, and without a guide. It's... nothing short of incredible."

"I haven't been able to do much of anything," Amara whispered, now staring at her hands.

Mom stood immediately and went to her, crouching down and covering Amara's hands with her own. "I believe that is my fault. Without a guide, without someone in the magical community to help, to show you the way, your magic would be hindered. But, there would be no way Cecilia would have been powerful enough to transport the three of you to another country without your magic, Amara. That was you, too."

Amara gave her a small smile, but I needed to keep going.

"So the two of us are potentially *more* powerful than Sonya and Seraphine. One witch that was kidnapped and drained, the other who lived her life in hiding. But who was also the last fated love our circle has seen."

Elodie nodded and jumped in as Mom went back to sit. "Sonya and Julian's story became almost like a fairytale. A story that mothers told their children at bedtime. A romance un-like any other, one that seemed almost impossible outside of books."

Xavier squeezed my hand tighter then, but otherwise didn't interject.

"Okay... so now what?" I asked. We had covered the fact that we were twins, powerful, our scars matched, and Xavier and I were... special.

"Three's a circle, Cecilia," Mom answered, a big grin on her face now. "Now, we resurrect our circle and fight against the Fallere's."

"Against Ezra."

Mom's smile dropped slightly. "Well—"

"She destroyed the ring." I jumped hearing Xavier's voice. Now he decided to speak? "Ezra's hunter ring. She destroyed it."

Mom whipped her head to Elodie so fast, her long, wavy mahogany hair almost hit her in the face. "That's not possible," they both said at the same time.

I shrugged. I didn't understand how people kept saying that when I physically saw it go up in flames and turn into ash.

"Ash? It turned into ash?" Mom asked when I told her what happened. Her brows crinkled and a frown replaced the smile. "El, the spell book. You said you had it?"

She nodded and went to the bedroom to grab it.

"Wait! The letter! Elodie, you have the box. I put Mom's letter back in it. What did it say?" I turned to Mom, obviously not needing to read it when she was right there.

The grin returned. "It told you all of this, sweet child. That you were powerful. You had a destiny larger than you could imagine. That you had a sister. About Elodie and Xavier. And, it reminded you that I loved you more than life itself. And you," she turned to Amara, "had a similar letter."

Her eyes lit up. "I did?"

Mom nodded. "Of course. I told your mother to give it to you whenever she felt the time was right. If she wanted. If you never developed your magic, then it would never need to be known. Your mother was an amazing woman to whom I owe *so* much."

Elodie returned with the spell book then and Mom flipped through it quickly, as if she knew exactly where she needed to find what she was looking for.

"I thought so," she muttered to herself. "Well, Cecilia, it's true. You are more powerful than Sonya. And Seraphine. Combined, most likely."

I gasped. I wasn't sure I wanted that responsibility. It seemed like a lot.

"It's okay. We're all here to help you. To guide you. You're strong and confident and capable of amazing things, Cecilia," Xavier whispered into my ear. The tickle of his breath made me shiver slightly. But, once again, his words and his voice instilled confidence in me. He lifted my hand and brushed his lips over my knuckles softly.

The necklace warmed against my skin. Or maybe it was the marking now permanently on my chest. Either way, between that and the ring on my finger, which I still didn't know anything about, a warmth spread through me, filling me with certainty.

With Xavier by my side, my newfound sister, my mother, and Elodie... I felt stronger than ever.

"Alright," I responded. "Where do we go from here?"

Mom smiled at me, like a proud mother. "We find more of the circle that's been in hiding. We resurrect our circle. We find our family."

Want a little more from Cecilia and Xavier?
Check out the bonus scene now at
www.authordaniellekeil.com/bonusscenes

Did you enjoy the Snap of Magic series? Make sure to drop a
review on Amazon or GoodReads today!

ABOUT THE AUTHOR

Danielle Keil grew up in the Chicagoland area. A recent transplant, she is enjoying the Mississippi life, especially the pool in her backyard.

Danielle has been happily married for over 10 years, and has two young children, a daughter and a son, who are exact replicas of her and her husband.

Danielle's love language is gifts, her Ennegram is 9w1, and she loves everything purple.

The way to her heart is through coffee, chocolate, and tacos(extra guac).

Want to hang out? Find her on Facebook, Instagram, or TikTok, or join the Dandelion family on Facebook.

Learn more at www.authordaniellekeil.com

Acknowledgements

Wow!!

I cannot believe the love for this series! You all jumped at the chance for these little witchy books and I so hope you've enjoyed them!

This series wouldn't have been possible at all without the amazing Amanda D. She was the one who I bounced ideas off of first, in the "this may never happen, but what about this idea" stage. Just know, if you ever want a book written by me, you should tell her your ideas so she can put them in my head!

Then the fantastic Emma Brown and her wonderful character art! When she told me she did the drawings on her Instagram posts, I was floored, and immediately asked if she did people. Was ASoM even a book yet? No. It was still an idea floating in my head. But she jumped at the chance and dealt with all of my changes and nonsense like a champ, producing the perfect Cecilia's for three books!

As always, my write-or-die's, Shain and Andrea, who held my hand and reminded me that every book is worth it and never to quit (literally, almost did quit before this series!).

And to you, my lovely, amazing, wonderful, fantastic readers. Thank you for taking a chance on this series and for loving on it so much! I'm so glad we went on this fun little adventure together and maybe we'll revisit Cecilia one day...